The arsonist cursed and tossed back a big gulp of whisky. The little bitch had survived once again. She was like a cat that just wouldn't run out of lives. Now, she had the townspeople cooing and cuddling her as if she were a toddler, for heaven's sake.

She'd ruined his life. Didn't anyone care about that? She had changed the long course of his time on this earth without a thought. Stealing his life, his love and his future should be cause for death, shouldn't it? The third time was supposed to be the charm, the final retribution.

And, now, just to make things worse, it seemed that she'd attracted the attention of the fire chief of all people. He was a good, hardworking man, Aaron, but she might lure him into taking her side in this war for supremacy. Isn't that what all women were born to do? They lured you, then left you with nothing.

## Praise for Dianne McCartney

Winner of Oklahoma Writers Federation Inc's 2022
Mystery/Suspense Novel Award

# Breathing Fire

## by

## Dianne McCartney

**Breathing Fire**

Cover Art by *Kim Mendoza*

The Wild Rose Press, Inc.
PO Box 708
Adams Basin, NY 14410-0708
Visit us at www.thewildrosepress.com

Publishing History
First Edition, 2023
Trade Paperback ISBN 978-1-5092-4934-3
Digital ISBN 978-1-5092-4935-0


Published in the United States of America

## Dedication

This book is dedicated to Ron Jollimore, my high school English teacher, who told me I should keep writing.

## Acknowledgments

A heartfelt thank you to my wonderful editor, Ally Robertson, and the rest of the terrific staff at The Wild Rose Press.

And, as always, thanks to my husband, Mitch, my daughter, Colleen, and my son-in-law, John, for their continual support.

Chapter One

Flames leapt from the corner of the room as he'd planned, ravenous destruction as his only goal. The burgeoning heat flared against his face and he reluctantly stepped back, out of harm's way. If he could dance in the devastation with her, he would, but as fate dictated, it wasn't his turn to die.

It was long past hers, however. Like a phoenix, she'd arisen from his other attempts, but this time, he'd made certain a violent, preemptive strike ensured she wouldn't survive. Triumph lay within his grasp. With a final adieu, he avoided the scattered debris and backed away. He pulled the heavy couch across the doorway and squeezed out the door. Padlocking it shut, he disappeared into the dark, beckoning shelter of the forest, hearing the fire cackle behind him like a dying witch.

Exhilarated, he ran with a triumphant laugh back to his lair just a few miles away, his fit legs carrying him along the familiar path. Search as the authorities might, they would never find him. Even though they often passed by, offering the smiles of the truly ignorant, they couldn't recognize the magnificent power which lay within. Hiding in plain sight had become his specialty. All the tears and drama that followed him were merely fodder for the future. Tragedy fed his insatiable need.

Just before he reached the relative safety of his abode, he heard the first screaming wail of a fire engine.

He knew who would be commanding the scene and laughed. Even the town's designated savior couldn't rescue her now.

\*\*\*\*

Against all odds, Harper Lindsay stirred. Oxygen-starved lungs had her sucking in a tortured breath. The horrifying nightmare seemed all too real. Throbbing pain made it feel as if someone had taken an ax to her head. She cried out, but the sound disappeared into the background of a threatening roar. Befuddled, she forced her eyelids open against the unexpected swell of heat. Her glazed vision finally focused enough to see basic shapes. Twelve feet away, a sheet of fire crackled and spit, voracious, gulping down the walls. A spark jumped and nibbled across one corner of the ceiling.

In panic, she pushed herself onto all fours. She fought for consciousness, her head swimming. *Why am I wet?* Wasting precious seconds touching her soaked blouse, she struggled to make sense of it. Sticky, pungent blood coated her.

She could see the barricaded doors and windows, battling blurry vision. *No time to wonder who did it.* She forced herself to focus and the terrible truth revealed itself. Only one option remained—to go up. The heavy rafters in the attic might allow her enough leeway to make it to the large window nestled inside the eaves if the stairs wouldn't disintegrate before she made it to the top. She lurched toward the steps as flames chased her, snapping at her heels. Dragging herself up by the railing, she suffered as the unprotected skin on her fingers blistered on the wrought iron surface. Sirens shrieking in the distance offered a shred of hope. *They're coming. They're coming for me.* Primal instinct warned her they wouldn't make it in time unless she made it to the window.

Staggering to the top of the stairs, she saw fire had already broken through in a nearby corner. She'd fall and be reduced to cinders if the ceiling collapsed. The wooden slats of the wall acted as an anchor to clutch onto as she edged her way to the opening, trembling so hard she lost her grip and fell to her knees twice. *Five feet to salvation.* Finally, she grabbed the metal opener at the base of the frame, burning her hands once more. Rusted, it wouldn't budge. Disbelief had her choking in a breath. *So close.* She sucked in smoke, coughing, as she sank to her knees. Her vision dimmed.

In one last, desperate attempt, she surged up and threw herself against the old, spider-webbed window. Feeling it shatter and scrape her body, she fell through. The ledge outside barely caught her as the salve of cold air embraced her skin. Her consciousness wavered as she wobbled to her feet, dimly hearing an answering cacophony of voices below. And, knowing she was finally free, she fell.

****

Aaron Lassiter had been certain Harper was trapped inside. As Fire Captain, he kept his crew outside of the disintegrating structure on arrival as the house couldn't be saved. Distraught, he realized no safe path existed for them to save her, either. On arrival, his firefighters stared in horror as the flames engulfed the house before leaping into action.

Moments later, a chorus of shouts erupted from the crowd. He whirled to see her figure teetering at the edge of the roof, the killing monster licking at her heels. Dashing forward a few seconds too late, he watched helplessly as she jumped or fell into the crowd below.

Two men standing beneath her broke her fall, linking arms in desperate partnership as she plummeted. All three hit the ground on impact. The two men scrambled aside to guarantee that Harper received immediate care. Aaron bellowed for the EMTs and stood aside as they fit an oxygen mask on her face. She had a gaping head injury, smoke inhalation, and blistered hands at the very least. "Harper." Raising his voice, he said her name, hoping for a verbal response when her eyelids fluttered.

Al Davis, the head medic, shook his head as he worked. "She's out, Chief. Her pulse is erratic. We need to go now." They lifted her on the gurney and trundled her to the ambulance, delivering her inside in a practiced move. With Al safely on board to treat her, the other man, Gary, ran to the driver's seat and jumped in before driving away. The blaring siren echoed a warning. They made the turn onto the main road as the vehicle's throaty acceleration signaled their ominous need for speed.

He and his men fought the flames for another thirty minutes, finally succeeding in containment, their only remaining option. Harper had lost everything but her life, assuming her injuries hadn't been worse than appeared. Confirmation from the ambulance team that Harper had safely arrived at the hospital and was under a doctor's care had relief passing through the ranks. Eventually, most of the watchers went home to bed, leaving his men to tend to the smoldering ashes. The charred remains would be too hot to ascertain the cause until tomorrow, but the ferocious nature of the fire made him suspicious.

The neighbors and their houses were safe, thank goodness. The country lots in this neighborhood were five acres apiece which allowed for privacy, and tonight, safety. Another hour later, he assigned a man to stand guard for the night and left a small tanker truck with him just in case of flare-ups. He sent the others back to the station. Their shift wasn't over until morning.

He made a stop at his house long enough to grab a restorative shower before he headed in to the hospital. His respect for Harper had only grown tonight. Most people, badly injured and gasping from the smoke, would have succumbed. What had it taken for her to dig deep and find the will to survive?

At 3:00 a.m., the halls of the county hospital were quiet. Becky Sherman came to the front desk as he approached. The middle-aged dynamo had managed the emergency department as long as he'd lived in Carlson, and apparently, years before that. A buxom brunette, she pushed her glasses up her nose, smothering a yawn. "Morning, Chief. Bet you're here to check in on the Lindsay girl."

"Yes. How's she doing?"

"Better. Dr. Farnum's in the ICU with her now. If you want to wait a few minutes, he can give you an update."

The so-called Intensive Care Unit was all of three beds, but it was enough to deal with the county's worst cases. Like most small, country hospitals, they functioned to stabilize all cases and solve lesser needs. If patients required more serious or long-term care, they were care-flighted an hour away to Fort Worth or Dallas. Luckily, this particular facility had an excellent standard of care.

On reaching the department, he waited outside the glassed-in walls, watching as the young doctor added notes to her chart. Harper seemed to be sleeping, likely knocked out from pain medication. Her pale face almost matched the white sheets tucked around her.

Dr. Farnum was the new medical resident, so he was the frequent recipient of the dreaded night shift. He was a welcome addition, well known for his calm and attentive nature. Dark-haired and serious, his black-framed glasses made him look like a super hero's alter ago. He wandered out the door, yawning, and caught Aaron's eye. "Good morning, Chief."

"Morning, Doc. How's she doing?"

A pleased expression crept onto his face. "Better. Things were a little dicey for a while. She's suffering from shock, but her pulse finally settled to a more reasonable rate."

"Can you tell me what her actual injuries are?"

Nodding, he said, "She gave me permission to tell you that before we gave her the sedatives. She has smoke inhalation, head trauma with level two concussion, a broken arm and two cracked ribs. Second degree burns on her hands, too." With a tired smile, he added, "She's strong, though. I think she's going to be fine. It could have been so much worse under the circumstances."

He felt a rush of relief that weakened his knees. "She's a damn titan. I still can't believe she dragged herself up those stairs and broke through the window."

"The head injury alone should have been enough to put her down. She said she's hard-headed. I'd say that's an understatement. It took twenty-two stitches to close." He shuffled, rubbing the shadowed circles under his eyes.

"Any way to tell what caused that? It seemed like an odd place to hit yourself accidentally."

"I thought so, too. By the time I thought to ask her, the drugs had already taken effect. Some sleep is the best thing for her right now."

He'd think more about that later. "Maybe she can tell us what happened when she wakes up."

The doctor nodded. "Said she has no family to come and help her, though. I guess the father deserted them and the mother's dead. No siblings."

"Don't worry. We'll take care of her." What he couldn't manage to take care of, others would. That was one of the benefits of living in a small town.

"Good. Thanks. That's one less thing to worry about." He sighed. "Well, I'm off to the break room for an hour or two. You heading out?"

"Nah, I'll sit with her for a while in case she wakes up."

"Doubtful, but do as you like. Having somebody nearby never hurts." He disappeared around the corner, shoulders slumped from fatigue.

Aaron entered the room and settled in the hard plastic chair by her bed, listening to the muted, reassuring beeps of the machines around her. She looked a shadow of her normal, vibrant self, her long, golden hair butchered by the charred hunks that had burned away and the unsightly band of stitches. He recalled the horrifying sight of her, staggering on the edge, before she plunged into the crowd. Framed by the flames, she'd looked like the stunt double from an action movie. It was a miracle that her clothes and hair had taken the brunt of the damage. If she'd been in a nightgown the outcome would have been tragic. And even two minutes later, he would have already pushed the desperate crowd back and no one would have been there to catch her.

Why had she been fully dressed in the middle of the night? Everyone knew she was a homebody, after all. Regardless, the blessing of the extra layers of heavy blue jeans, a sweatshirt and jacket had saved her. He wondered what she'd hit her head on to cause such an injury. Maybe she would remember, maybe not. With an injury of that size and amount of blood, it hadn't been a light blow, that was for sure.

Unable to rest, he mulled about her situation for the next few hours. At one point, she mumbled, so he stood and leaned over to hear her words. "Aaron," she whispered, stunning him. He put a careful hand on her shoulder. "I'm here." His words did the trick. Calming, she slipped back into deep sleep.

A month ago, he'd asked her out to dinner and been disappointed when she offered what was clearly an excuse and begged off. He didn't understand why because he knew how to read when a woman was attracted to him and she'd displayed the right signs. There was no other man hanging around her as far as he could tell. Other than running her furniture upcycling business, she tended to rely on the local children and the elderly for company. Why that was, he didn't know. He'd read the attraction between them, but she seemed resolute about staying away. Her choice, of course, but her decision disappointed him.

At 6:30 a.m., the busy hospital came back to life, the rattling of trays a sign of coming breakfast. When the clock hit 7:00 a.m., Becky showed up, offering a sympathetic smile. "Brought you a bite to eat." She handed him a cup of coffee and two banana muffins.

"Bless you," he said, digging in at once, his stomach grumbling.

"Miz Mason called to say that the female hospital volunteers are going to take turns sitting with her, so, don't worry, she won't be left alone. They'll get started on finding a place for her to stay, too, until she can find someplace new to rent."

"No need to look for a rental. I've got that caretaker's cottage at my place she can have. It's not fancy, but it'll do the trick for now."

"You're a good man, Aaron. She'll appreciate your thoughtfulness."

"It's the least I can offer her after what she's been through. Hopefully, it'll help her get back on her feet." Standing, he tried to stretch the kinks out of his neck. He tried rubbing it with one hand, but that didn't help either. Plastic chairs weren't made for tall men. As they stood talking, volunteer Bernice Talbot appeared and shooed him away, taking his place at Harper's bedside.

"We'll call you if she wakes up." She settled and pulled her knitting out of her bulky tote bag, her thin body fitting in the chair better than his did. Since the woman had raised six children of her own, he felt confident Harper would be in reliable hands.

Exhaustion tried to beckon him to bed, but he persevered and drove back to what used to be Harper's place. He told Fred Landry, the fireman who'd stayed on guard duty all night, to go home. Standing far back, he looked over the depressing ruins. The fire had burned too fast and too hot to be an accident. Even though the house had been made of wood, it had been a sturdy old place. They should have been able to save at least part of it, especially since they'd made it there seven minutes after a neighbor reported seeing smoke as he drove past. Any longer might have meant certain death for Harper.

It would be a few more frustrating hours before the steaming ashes cooled enough to allow him to investigate. A small-town department like theirs didn't have the resources to have a licensed fire investigator, but he'd taken a few classes that would help him make an initial inspection and shoot some pictures. After that, he would record it all and send it to a state fire investigator in Dallas who would help make a determination about the cause as a favor.

He heard the clattering sound of tires on gravel and looked up to see the local sheriff pulling up. Ty Randall had been out of town with his wife last night, but his subordinate had been on scene to help. His tall, fit, friend climbed out, paused to look, and ran a hand through his cropped blond hair. A former Marine, he understood duty more than most. He strode over, his face creased with concern. "Well, son of a bitch. I heard it was bad, but the whole damn thing's gone."

He nodded. "It was a near thing. Harper was lucky to get out."

"It's a miracle, really. They told me she took a dive off the roof and a couple of guys broke her fall." He came to stand next to him. "I heard you got there quickly and it was still too late. You figure it's arson?"

"The embers are still too hot to get in there and check things out, but I'd bet on it. It burned way quicker than it should have otherwise. I'd be happy to be proven wrong, but I don't think we'll get that lucky."

"Damn, Aaron. We haven't had anything but accidental fires here in at least a decade. As far as I know, anyway. Why would anybody want to burn down this old place?"

As they stood discussing possible scenarios, Arne

Jackson, the owner of the property, yanked his truck to a stop. He jumped out and slammed the door, stomping over to join them. His clenched lips demonstrated the anger he would feel obliged to act on. "What the hell happened here? I don't get a call until an hour ago?"

Used to dealing with the public, Ty kept his voice low and soothing. "Wasn't much point in waking you in the middle of the night, Arne, and we were plenty busy. Nothing left for any of us to do but wait for the cinders to cool so Aaron can take a look."

The older man fumed, his cheeks getting redder by the minute. "I'll bet that little bitch left the damn stove on or let a cigarette drop into that mess of junk she likes to collect."

Aaron knew from personal experience the man was difficult to tolerate at the best of times. "Watch your damn language. Harper almost died in the fire. She had to jump off the roof to get clear and she's stuck in the hospital with injuries for a few days at least."

Instead of that putting things in perspective, his face graduated to near purple color. "Well, that's not my fault and she better not imply that it was. I keep all my properties in tiptop condition. She better not imply that I don't." He made it sound like he was the king of real estate. He only had two rental properties, not twenty, but he loved to exaggerate his wealth.

"No one's saying any different," Ty said. "Talk to your insurance company about it. Aaron will have more of an idea what happened in the next few days."

"I'm not paying for a hotel for her, either. She can hole up on someone else's dime."

Aaron sucked back the urge to knock a little sense into him. The discipline cost him. He was old-fashioned enough to believe that men should always look out for women. "No need to worry about that," he said, knowing this awful man never would. "The ladies from the hospital auxiliary and I will be honored to take care of Harper."

Even that promise failed to keep him happy. "How about all that wood and crap she has stored in my shed?"

He glared at Arne, having reached his boiling point. "I'd bet she's paid to the end of the month, at least, so she has a legal right to leave it there for now. And I'm sure she'll be glad to hear how concerned you are for her welfare."

Ty hustled the arrogant man away in an obvious effort to keep the peace. After Arne's truck pulled out, his friend came walking back. "I need to get back to the station and see what else I missed. Let me know if you need some help."

"Will do." Thank God for Ty, whose natural patience and humor were essential in a small-town department. The two of them shared a respect for their community and a love of serving a sometimes-unappreciative public. Thank goodness, they didn't have too many citizens as selfish as Arne, who was probably the least-liked man in town.

Three hours later, the accumulated mounds of ashes had cooled enough to allow a serious investigation. It didn't take long for him to discover the five different points of origin for the fire. Those five areas were the blackest of all which told him all he needed to know. Hot spots were evident in each of the four corners of the living room and in the center. Someone had wanted to guarantee that this house burnt to the ground. Accelerants had clearly been used, probably gasoline by the smell of it. The remains of a sofa blocked the door and he found a metal padlock on the ground nearby. He took careful photos of each section, then a sweeping record of the entire room, or rather, the floor, about all that was left. There was no question in his mind that the evidence left behind spelled a clear intent to harm.

*Damn it.* Who would want to hurt Harper? Had they known she was home or did they just consider her collateral damage? Either way, it alarmed him.

He spent another exhausting hour sifting through the piles of ashes, but didn't catch sight of anything new that would provide more information. As he was winding up the investigation, his cellphone rang. It was one of the nurses at the hospital; Harper was awake and asking for him. After calling another man to stand guard in his place, he drove to see her. Promising himself some sleep after he was done talking to her, he hauled himself out of his truck and went through the sliding glass doors. When he reached her room, he found her awake, slumped to one side of the bed and staring at the ceiling. "Good morning," he said, feeling his heart stutter in relief. She looked pale and shaky, but almost normal, despite all the cuts and bruises. Her current appearance probably scandalized her but it reassured him.

"Hi." Her husky voice scratched out and she cleared her throat to try again. The strain was evident. It sounded as if she'd been shouting for days. "I hope I didn't disturb your work."

"No, I was glad to hear you were awake. I'd just finished examining what's left at your place."

"Not much, right?"

She sounded so glum, his empathy rose. "I'm afraid not. At least the flames didn't reach the shed, so at least

13

your materials are safe." It was the only thing he thought might cheer her.

Tears gathered in the corners of her eyes, but she brushed them impatiently away with her forearm. "I remembered something I need to tell you. Something from last night. It's important."

"Okay. Go ahead."

She sucked in a breath and met his gaze. "Someone hit me before the fire started."

Chapter Two

Aaron pulled the spare chair over beside the bed so she wouldn't have to crane her neck to meet his gaze. Settling into it, and ignoring his exhausted muscles, he said, "Tell me everything you remember that happened before the fire."

"I was working in the shed until around midnight. When I finished, I locked the door behind me and walked across the lawn." She shut her eyes as if picturing it. "I remember the key turning the lock, but, just as I stepped through the doorway, someone shoved me in the back. Right after that, terrible pain seemed to blast in my head out of nowhere. That's all that I registered, not any weapon. Just before I passed out, I heard him say one word." She huffed in a breath. "Bitch."

"You said him. Are you sure it was a man?"

"I didn't see him, but the voice was definitely male."

"Did anything seem familiar about it?"

"No. I'm sorry. All I remember is that his tone was deep and angry."

He removed his cellphone from his pocket and tapped one familiar number.

"What are you doing?" She brushed her hair out of her eyes, her hand trembling.

"Calling Ty. He'll need to take your statement."

She frowned. "But I didn't see anything. Not really."

"Doesn't matter, honey. We need to get this into a

report and figure out what's going on." He caught his friend in the neighborhood and he said he'd be right over. When Aaron glanced back at her, her face had turned red. "Are you okay?"

"I lost everything." She rambled on about her confusion about what happened and he let her, knowing she had to talk about it to get it out of her system. They'd piece things together after Ty arrived.

He didn't want her to be stressed out and reassured her that they would help her get everything organized. In an attempt to distract her, he asked, "Have you got renter's insurance?"

"Y-yes."

"Okay, well, that's a start. At least that'll be enough cash to get you set up with essentials again. And the shed wasn't touched, so, like I said, you still have your tools and stock. That's a good starting point."

"That's true, I guess." She sighed. "I loved living in that old house, even though Arne's a jerk for a landlord. That's no surprise. There are hardly any decent rentals around here, though, and I'd rather not rent from him again."

"I had an idea about that." He heard Ty striding down the hall, greeting one of the nurses outside the door. "Tell Ty everything you can remember and we'll discuss it after he leaves."

The sheriff entered, his hat twisting in his fingers. "Good morning, you two. Harper, I hear you have some details from last night to share with me." He took a seat, whipping a small notepad from his pocket and writing down what she said. When she finished speaking, he asked, "Do you know of anyone who would want to hurt you?"

She shook her head and winced from the effort. "I pretty much keep to myself."

"Any angry ex-boyfriends?"

"No. I don't really date." He saw the same question in Ty's eyes that was rolling around in his head. *Why the hell not?*

"Anybody around here ask you for a date and you turned them down?"

Her gaze flew to his own, and he understood her dilemma. "Tell him. It's okay."

"Ah, Aaron asked me." She fidgeted, then took a moment to get more comfortable. "And Arne. And Fred, down at the grocery. And the Davis boy—what's his name King. I think that's everyone."

*Good Lord.* Talk about running the gambit. The Davis boy was maybe twenty-five at best and Arne was around sixty. He and Fred fell almost halfway in between. Now, he understood why Arne'd been such an ignorant tool. She'd turned him down and his over-inflated ego couldn't take it. Probably thought his money would persuade her to ignore the fact he was old enough to be her father. Aaron knew her enough to know that was hogwash. She didn't seem to care anything about the financial hierarchy in town, thank goodness, unlike a few he could name.

With no more information forthcoming, Ty made his retreat, promising to drop by again later in case she remembered anything else. After he left, Aaron could tell she was running out of steam already. Her eyes were at half-mast. "You need some more sleep. The nurses will smack me around if I tucker you out."

She started to protest and he ignored her. "I don't want you to worry about a place to stay, though. I have a caretaker's cottage on my land you're more than welcome to use. It's not fancy, but I think you'd like it."

Her eyes widened. "But I have all my stock, too. I'll have to find a place for that by the end of the month."

"No worries. That gives us two weeks to move it. I have a big, new barn that's only half full. You're welcome to keep it in there for now."

She stared at him. "Why are you being so nice to me?" she whispered.

They could discuss his personal interest in her later. She had enough to deal with right now. "Because I'd like to think we're friends and I want to help." He patted her shoulder. "Now, get some rest. They won't release you for at least a couple of days, so we have time to figure it all out together."

He left her in the care of Thelma Banks, one of the local women. Things were quiet at the station, so he headed back out to the fire site. Now that he had recorded all the evidence and still waited for his friend's input about arson, he could release the site to Arne. As he turned into the paved driveway, he could see the man already here arguing with the firefighter Aaron had posted there to guard the place. He sighed as he shut off the engine. It was going to be another long day.

The older man stomped over to meet him before he even had the chance to shut the door. His salt and pepper hair stood up in every direction, as agitated as he seemed to be at the moment. "I told your lackey—"

"Arne, you don't have the right to enter until I give you permission. You certainly don't command my firefighters. They only answer to me, not you."

Bristling, he stuck his jaw out. "I told the insurance people they could get in to take pictures today." He crossed his arms, his forearms so tense you could bounce a quarter off them.

"You should have checked with me first." When the other man started to interrupt, he put a hand up to stop his tirade. "As it happens, that's why I'm here. I took recordings and photographs of all the evidence earlier today, so I'll allow the adjustors in to have a look around. Just remind them not to touch anything. And the same goes for you."

He shut his mouth, robbed of his reason to continue complaining. Never one to stay happy for long, he gestured at the shed. "How about getting access to my outbuilding?"

This part of things allowed him a mean little thrill of pleasure. "Harper confirmed she is still paid to the end of the month. Her inventory will be moved before then."

He growled, "It's just a stupid pile of trash. Can't I just put it out on the curb for the garbage men to pick up?"

"No, you can't. It might seem like trash to you, but it's her livelihood. You've already been paid for the space. I can get Ty to explain how the law works to you if need be." He made a mental note to move her items as soon as possible to prevent Arne breaking in and doing God knows what to her merchandise.

He cursed. "What did you find out about the origin of the fire?"

Until he had his suspicions verified, he didn't plan on sharing any details with this jerk. "Too early to say for certain. I'm not making any determination until I receive the official report from the state investigator." He waved a hand toward the burn site. "I wouldn't venture inside until your insurance representative shows up."

Leaving the man mumbling to himself, he dismissed the fireman who'd been standing guard. Another walk around the site didn't yield anything else, so he headed home to catch up on a few hours' sleep before returning to the station. Back at home, he set his phone alarm and dove onto the bed, stretching to fill the space. It occurred to him that he wouldn't allow his work responsibilities to consume so much of his time if he had someone waiting at home.

After he went back to work, the usual grind of paperwork and scheduling took up the final hours of the workday. Mid-afternoon, he received the call that confirmed his suspicions. The familiar burn patterns and the other evidence spelled arson. He was thankful for the speediness of the report. As he sat mulling over his next steps he should take, he heard a rap on the office door. Looking up, he saw through the glass insert it was Ty. Waving him in, he said, "Come on in. I didn't expect to see you so soon."

The other man settled in the opposite chair, stretching his long legs out in front of him with a sigh. "Discovered something interesting I need to run past you."

"I was just going to call you anyway. My contact in the city just confirmed our suspicions. The fire was arson."

"Damn it. Can't say I'm surprised, but I was hoping we were both wrong."

"No such luck, I'm afraid. What did you need to see me about?"

"Just came from checking in with Harper. She was feeling stronger, so we had a little talk."

"She's feeling better? Good. Did she remember

anything else?"

"No, but she told me something else which surprised the heck outta me. She said that she guessed she and fire just didn't get along."

Her words struck him as a little strange, but he knew she still felt out of sorts. "What did she mean by that?"

"Apparently, she's been in not one, but two previous fires."

Statistically, he knew that was highly unusual. "You're kidding. When? Recently?"

Ty shook his head. "No, I guess the first one happened when she was ten. She almost got caught in the middle of a forest fire when she was with friends. She ran in to save a dog that someone had tied to a tree and almost didn't make it back out."

"And the second time?"

"A car fire when she was twenty-three. She was driving home from a party late one night and the whole dashboard of her car went up in flames. Good reflexes meant she was able to pull off the highway and dive out in time, but the car was totally destroyed."

Intuition had him considering several different possibilities. "Did the investigators figure out the cause of either one?"

"Nothing on the first one. I guess on the second their best guess was an electrical short. Sounds like a shot in the dark to me. Didn't appear that there was much of an official investigation."

He tried to ignore the sick, churning feeling in his gut. "An arsonist wouldn't be able to wait that long in between attacks, would he? She's thirty-four. We're talking over a decade between incidents."

"I don't see how, but we can't ignore the

improbability of one woman barely escaping three fires."
He met his gaze. "She has no alibi for the time before
this fire. She said she was working on her projects in the
shed, but there's no one to verify her actions."

He clenched his fists at his insinuation as anger
simmered. "You can't believe she had anything to do
with this. She has nothing to gain and the flames could
have burned her to death."

"I've never seen any sign that she isn't just what she
appears to be—a lovely, kind young woman. But I have
to look into the other fires, regardless. We can't afford to
ignore any possibilities, no matter how remote."

"I know, but it's a waste of time."

"Don't look so put out. I'll keep anything I discover
quiet and I don't expect to find anything. We just have
to cover our bases." He made a speedy exit soon
afterward, leaving Aaron to brood. If anyone got wind of
her being associated with those other fires, tongues
would wag. Vicious people existed everywhere and her
reputation could be damaged.

****

The arsonist cursed and tossed back a big gulp of
whisky. The little bitch had survived once again. She was
like a cat that just wouldn't run out of lives. Now, she
had the townspeople cooing and cuddling her as if she
were a toddler, for heaven's sake.

She'd ruined his life. Didn't anyone care about that?
She had changed the long course of his time on this earth
without a thought. Stealing his life, his love and his
future should be cause for death, shouldn't it? The third
time was supposed to be the charm, the final retribution.

And now, just to make things worse, it seemed that
she'd attracted the attention of the fire chief of all people.

He was a good, hardworking man, Aaron, but she might lure him into taking her side in this war for supremacy. Isn't that what all women were born to do? They lured you, then left you with nothing. If she did that to Aaron, he might have to die alongside her. It wasn't the path he, himself, would have chosen, but it might become the ultimate cost.

He slumped down into his favorite chair to mull over his dwindling options.

Chapter Three

First thing in the morning, Aaron went for a long run in an attempt to clear his head. The clear, sunny day was a soothing tonic and he stayed to the outskirts of town, so no one would flag him down to chat. Last night's dreams had been full of both flames and erotic thoughts about Harper, a convoluted combination only a firefighter might understand. There was more than one kind of fiery heat, after all. As he cooled down on his way back to the house, he decided to go and talk to her before showing up at the station. Enjoying a long, cool shower and putting on fresh clothes put him in a better frame of mind. When he arrived at the hospital, he found her alone, having just finished what she wanted of her breakfast. It wasn't enough to keep a squirrel alive, but he'd worry about ensuring she was well-fed later. "Good morning," He stepped inside.

A smile lifted the corners of her lips. "Hi." Today, she had some color in her cheeks, a change from the pale complexion she'd sported yesterday. Her voice sounded stronger as well.

"How are you feeling?"

"A lot better, thanks. I told them I felt healthy enough to leave, but they don't seem too convinced."

Aaron could understand how she felt. He didn't like being penned inside, either. "You've been through a lot. They don't want to hurry you, then have you pass out or something and have to come back. Don't rush it."

"I guess you're right." She didn't look like the prospect pleased her.

He took the visitor's seat and decided to dive right into what might be an awkward subject. "Ty told me you've been in a fire before. Two, in fact."

She nodded. "He said that's really rare."

"Yes, it is."

Meeting his gaze, she said, "I know Ty has to look into everything, but I didn't have anything to do with this, you know. Why would I? I almost didn't make it out."

Her words rang true. Instead of making light of her concerns, he addressed them. She was smart and practical, so he saw no need to treat her like a child. "Ty has to check out all possibilities for the official record. He doesn't think you did it. Neither do I. But it seems very unlucky that you've had this happen a lot more than statistics would say is natural."

She gulped and looked away. "When I was younger, I used to think someone was out to get me." Her embarrassed tone made him sympathize with her. "Sometimes, I still have nightmares about that. I know it sounds a little crazy."

"We'll have to check out that possibility, too." He wanted her to understand they were on her side, ready to protect her.

Yanking her gaze back to his, she stuttered, "R-really?"

"Yes." He put a gentle hand on her arm to calm her. "It's probably nothing, but we have to be sure. Is there anyone from all those years back that you've had problems with?"

"They were just dreams. I thought I was paranoid. Most of the time, I never believed they had any basis in fact." She shrugged. "I don't have any enemies that I'm aware of. What on earth could I have done to provoke something vengeful, like burning everything to the ground? Especially when I didn't even own the house."

"I can't say. But, promise me you'll give it some serious thought. Try to think about anyone, man or woman, who just creeped you out or tried to cause trouble for you."

"Okay. I'll try." Sighing, she rubbed her face. "Is Arne being a pain about all this?"

Not wanting to worry her, he said, "Oh, no more than usual."

"That's not saying much. He's always so hard to deal with." She twisted her fingers together, shifting her cast. "Do you think my stock is safe in his shed?"

"I spoke to him about that and reminded him that you're paid to the end of the month. Within the next few days, I'll get some of the guys from the station to help and we'll move it all to my barn, okay?"

"I'll owe you, big time."

"Make me a nice dinner when you're feeling better and we'll call it even."

Her cheeks flushed. "Okay."

Her easy agreement to his suggestion made him smile. Maybe going through this drama together would help her be more comfortable around him. He excused himself when Dr. Mason came to the door, rapping against the door surround. "Oh, hello, Aaron. Am I interrupting? I'm just here to check up on our girl."

"That's fine, Doc. I have to get to work, anyway." In his early sixties, the silver-haired physician looked like a poster boy for his profession in his crisp white coat and slim build. His gaze flitted back and forth between the two of them, clearly curious. He was a long-time resident, but Aaron didn't know him well. Bidding them goodbye, he headed for the station.

The department had three brush fires to beat into submission that day, the too-dry summer taking its toll on nature. Luckily, they were all small and easily controlled. The last man returned to the station at six thirty and Aaron headed home. After showering and changing, he walked up to the caretaker's cottage, situated a hundred yards behind his house. When he opened the front door, the interior smelled musty from the building being closed up for so long. Now that the temperature had cooled, he decided to open the windows and air the cottage out while he prepared the place for his guest. He always kept the water, heat and electricity on because sometimes one of his men needed a place to stay.

Having forgotten to grab fresh linens for the bed, he walked back to the house. On his return, he noticed the towels in the closet smelled musty, so he replaced them, too. By the time he'd finished puttering back and forth, the air smelled fresher inside, so he closed the place up again. Other than a few groceries he'd pick up tomorrow to fill the shelves and refrigerator, Harper should have all the basics she needed.

As he walked back down the hill, he remembered Harper would need clothing. *Damn it.* She wouldn't have anything to wear and she could hardly leave the hospital wearing an open-back gown. Back in the house, he picked up his phone and called Ty's wife, Sandra. He explained the problem, startled when she laughed.

"Don't panic. You won't have to go shopping. Ty already asked if I could pick her up a few changes of clothes along with toiletries and stuff. I'll do it first thing in the morning."

"Bless you two. I'll pay you back."

"Don't be silly. We're happy to help a neighbor. Do you need any help preparing the cottage?"

"I just aired it out and put fresh linens on the beds and in the bathroom. Tomorrow, I'll buy her enough groceries to keep her going for a while. After that, we should be all set."

"Is she being released tomorrow? I heard she's doing better than expected."

"Tomorrow or the next day. They'll decide in the morning." Crisis averted, they said their good nights.

\*\*\*\*

After eating an early dinner, Harper lay, fidgeting, in her hospital bed. She would have been totally overwhelmed if it hadn't been for Aaron, Ty, Sandra and all of the volunteers. When her worries became too much, she just made another list to organize her thoughts, something at which she excelled. The staff had provided her with a pencil and a pad. Number one of the things to be grateful for was that she'd survived. The burns on her hands still hurt like hell, even with the ointment and bandages. Her head was better as long as she didn't move quickly or too much. At least she'd broken her left arm, not her right, so she could manage with just her dominant hand. Her ribs still hurt every time she breathed, but they were slowly getting better. Dr. Mason said it would take some time, that it was important not to rush things. The ladies had chopped her hair off at her shoulders to get rid of most of the ugly, charred sections, but at least it would be easier to maintain. The only thing she was a little vain about, her hair would at least grow back.

When the nurses helped her up to walk twice a day, she still wobbled. Up and down the brightly lit hall they walked her, with her shaking like a terrified toddler. Embarrassing, true, but they said it was just because she'd been in bed so much and that it would take some time to rebuild her energy and her muscles. Each day, she got a little stronger. At least they allowed her to go to the bathroom now, instead of using a rather undignified bedpan. Sandra had called to discuss picking up clothes for her and she asked for sweats and T-shirts, so she could pull them on herself. Asking for help dressing would mortify her.

She couldn't believe Aaron was going to allow her to live in his cottage while she recovered. He wouldn't hear of her paying rent when she'd mentioned it, but she'd tried to convince him otherwise. Paying her own way was part of her code for self-reliance. She'd have to think of a way to pay him back.

Turning him down when he'd asked her out had been a form of self-protection. She'd always struggled with dating relationships and knew she'd blunder through it, embarrassing herself. For the first time in years, she'd been tempted, though. He showed patience, humor and kindness to everyone around him and that was attractive enough. Add his dark looks and big, fit body to those qualities, and he was a real temptation, that's for sure. What would it be like living so close to him, even for a little while? And where would she find another decent rental?

With a sigh, she realized she was just stressing

herself out unnecessarily. *Just take one step at a time.* She had a safe place to stay. Ty's sweet, funny wife had been so friendly and kind, she hoped they could become friends. And soon, she could get back to her creations and start making money again. It hardly seemed like work because she loved her job. It's true she had no family to care about her, but she had a few good friends here and had made many more since the fire. She would manage just fine. Trying to ignore the sounds of people passing in the hall, she laid her head down, snuggling into her pillow, and closed her eyes.

****

Harper was released from the hospital at four o'clock the next day. Sandra had offered to drive her to the cottage, so Aaron wouldn't have to take time off from work. She texted him to let him know that, after signing the required slew of release papers, she was now resting at the cottage. Meeting them there when he left work at five, he found the two women curled into the old, flowered armchairs in the small living room. Half-empty glasses sat on the table between them. Harper wore new clothes, made obvious by telling creases in the material. "You get settled in okay?"

"Yes, she did," Sandra replied. "But she's getting sleepy again and is just too nice to ask me to leave."

Dark circles showed her fatigue from even that amount of exertion. Harper's cheeks flushed as her gaze met his. "I really appreciate how kind everyone has been. I don't know how I'd manage without you all."

Ty's wife got to her feet and stretched, patting her shoulder. "We're glad to help. I'd better run, though. If Ty comes home to no dinner, he gets grumpy faster than a sleepy two-year-old."

"Tell him to cook for himself," Aaron teased. "I'm sure it's way past his turn."

She shook her head. "That wouldn't yield an appetizing result, I promise you. He used to try and cook when we first got married and it wasn't a pretty picture. That man can burn water." She turned to Harper. "Call if you need anything, you hear? Anything at all. We're only ten minutes away."

"I will. Thanks again." With a cheery wave, she was gone. After the front door thumped closed, the soft murmur of her hybrid car retreated.

He faced Harper. "Tell me the truth. Which do you want first, dinner or bed?"

"Sleep first, I think." Standing, she yawned. "I feel as weak as a kitten. To be honest with you, it's a little embarrassing."

"Will you be okay moving around the house without assistance?"

"Yes, I'll just take my time and use the walls for support if I have to."

"I assume Sandra showed you the bedroom and everything else you might need?"

"Yes, thanks. She took care of everything." She appreciated that he watched her carefully, but didn't hover over her. Always wanting to be independent meant having people take care of her took some getting used to, unfortunately.

"Okay, good. Why don't you call me when you wake up? I'll bring you up some dinner. I put my number in the phone we bought you."

"You don't have to do that. I don't expect you to wait on me, for heaven's sake. I can manage. I already saw all the food in the cupboards."

"You shouldn't be using that left arm to do much of anything, especially for the first few days. The doctors won't be too happy if you make your problems worse." He shrugged. "I have to cook for myself anyway. It's no problem."

"Well, then, thanks. I appreciate it." Watching until she hobbled down the hall and disappeared through the bedroom door, he let himself out, closing the front door behind him.

**\*\*\*\***

Harper never even made it under the bedcovers. Easing herself down, she lay on top and pulled a pillow under her head. That was all she remembered. When she woke at 8:00 p.m. and called, Aaron brought her some chicken vegetable casserole that smelled much better than the hospital food she'd been eating. Bidding her to sit at the table, he scooped a hefty portion onto her plate and served her. While she ate, he told her about his day at work, giving her some insight into his responsibilities. He even rinsed the dishes off after she ate. Before she toddled off to bed, he saw her to her room and let himself out, locking the place behind him.

They settled into an easy routine over the next few days. Aaron would check on her before he left in the morning and, as soon as he came home, he made them dinner. During the day, frequent visitors dropped by to keep her company, mostly women from town who wanted to offer support in one form or another. Some of them brought simple food she could eat for lunch. Another few said they could run her to and from her doctor's appointments. For someone who spent so much of her time alone, their company was a welcome surprise. She didn't know how she'd ever pay them back.

Aaron and three of his men moved her construction supplies into the barn after work the third day after her release from the hospital. Big surprise, they received no thank you from Arne for removing it ahead of the deadline. He hadn't made any friends over the callous way he'd treated Harper, but Aaron doubted he cared a whit.

They weren't any closer to finding their arsonist, much to his chagrin. No one had seen anyone near her place that night and no one had bought any extra gas they couldn't explain. In the city, there'd be the possibility of security cameras, but people were old school around here. Security usually came in the form of a couple of dogs or a shotgun. That and their community watch program scared off most of the trouble makers.

On the positive side, he and Harper were getting a lot more comfortable around each other. They usually ate dinner together and walked around his field for exercise afterward so she could regain her strength. The first night they tried, she only made it about a hundred steps, but she'd improved a lot after that. He suspected she exercised a little during the day to help her muscles recover. Tonight, they'd looked at her projects in the barn and she told him about her plans for each one. He found himself oddly impressed. She had a way of transforming things and giving them new life. It was ironic since he felt oddly transformed around her, but that was a subject for another day.

Two weeks after the accident, Harper had an appointment at the hospital to have her arm x-rayed. They took the x-ray as soon as she arrived. After a fifteen-minute wait, the technician reported that the doctor had examined the x-ray and said it was healing well. They could give her a shorter cast that was easier to maneuver in. When the tech had finished making the necessary adjustments, Dr. Mason came in to talk to her. He held out the x-ray for her to view, pointing out the mending break. "As you can see, you have some healing already which is what we hoped for. Don't overdo it, though. When you're totally healed, we'll arrange for some physiotherapy appointments for you."

"When do you think it will be healed?" She didn't want to be pushy, but she was anxious for life to get back to normal.

He gave a practiced smile. "Another four weeks would be my best bet, but we'll have to wait and see. After we remove the cast, the physiotherapist will guide you through some exercises to help you regain flexibility. I know with your...occupation...that's somewhat important."

She was used to the patronizing air when people talked about her job, so she ignored it, offering a cheery smile. "That sounds great. Thanks."

"Do you have any other questions?"

"No. I think I'm good."

Nodding, he said, "Feel free to call the office if anything comes up. Otherwise, we'll plan to check it in a month and see where we stand." He left, his gaze once again focused on the chart in his hand.

She was glad to have someone knowledgeable to oversee her recovery. Dr. Mason was the senior doctor around here and everyone seemed to respect him, even though he wasn't the friendliest man around. Good looking for an older man, she'd heard he was single but had never seen him out with anyone. She couldn't talk— it's not like she was a party animal. The very idea of that made her laugh as she went to meet today's chauffeur for a ride home.

\*\*\*\*

When the arsonist heard whose house Harper was recuperating at, he cursed. How in hell would he get access to her with a vigilant man like Aaron standing guard? Far too bright for this town, Aaron had appeared out of nowhere, pleasing the local ladies no end. He wondered why in hell he didn't try for a job in the city. What was the appeal of a small town like this unless you'd grown up here as he, himself, had?

The added complication wouldn't stop him, of course. It would just take some extra thought to find a way around his guarded nature. Was he enamored with her? That had to be it. Chasing women was, after all, the main pre-occupation of most young men. Aaron was almost too good to be true. With his tall, dark figure, a good job and a home, he made an excellent target for the local women. He hadn't fallen prey to anyone so far, though, but certainly not because there hadn't been attempts. The local women remained, by and large, frustrated by his seeming lack of interest.

The fire chief would surely grow bored with Harper after a while. Along with her so-called job and her love of books, she didn't do much with her time other than some volunteer work. He'd never heard of her attending the usual outings at local bars and sporting events. Too bad, because that scenario would have offered endless opportunities to take advantage. Despite that beautiful bank of long, blonde hair, she didn't seem to have what it took to hang onto a man.

Maybe he should just wait until she was left alone once again. And, then, he'd pay her a final visit. A memorable one that would finally put an end to the woman whose presence tortured him.

Chapter Four

On Friday night, Harper enjoyed a late dinner with Aaron on the sprawling, wooden deck built on the back of his house. Afterward, they sat and discussed how they'd spent the quiet week. The night sky was clear and full of brilliant stars, the early autumn winds still for a change. As fall arrived, the frequent grass fires died down due to fewer campers and thank heaven, they had seen no reoccurrence of their arsonist's perverse games. Leaning back against the back of her chair, her belly full of a little too much dinner, she stifled a yawn. "I'm sorry. I guess it's time for me to hit the hay. I haven't gone to bed so early since I was a kid."

"I'll walk you back." He stood and leaned down to offer her a hand. Her casted arm made her clumsy, but he never made her feel that way. Being quietly helpful was more his style.

"Oh, you don't need to escort me. It's what—a few hundred feet?" She took hold of him with her good hand, letting his strong hand and arm do some of the work of getting her safely to her feet. She teetered for a moment, giggling.

"Steady there." Once she regained her balance, they began to walk. "My mother taught me to always see a woman to her front door. She'd say that's Manners 101."

She glanced up at him and smiled. "Well, we wouldn't want to get you in trouble with your mom, would we?"

"No, ma'am, you wouldn't." Following her down the steps, he gestured for her to keep going. "We used to have to pay a quarter into a jar every time we cussed. At one point, she claimed she paid the entire mortgage with my help." Despite the teasing, Harper could tell he had something else on his mind. She paused when they reached her door and swung around to face him. He cleared his throat. "Can I ask you a question?"

"Of course. You can ask me anything you want."

"It doesn't really matter in the whole scheme of things. I'm just curious. Why wouldn't you have dinner with me that time I asked you? You know—about two weeks before the fire."

She felt her cheeks flush and hoped it was too dark for him to notice. Just for once, she wished her face didn't give every single thing away. He deserved the truth, though. Sighing, she admitted, "I'm just so bad at dating. Honestly, if there was a dating school, I'd be the one with a dunce cap on my head every single year."

Laughing, he said, "Oh, come on. You can't be that bad. You're attractive, well-spoken and you've got an interesting job. You're the gold standard for women in my book."

She'd never been anyone's gold standard before and couldn't quell the rush of pleasure his words made her feel. "Thanks for the compliment, but I guess I feel like a fraud sometimes. Makeup, finding the right dress, all of that just seems like a big waste of time to me. I'd rather be reading or creating a new piece of furniture." She groaned. "I know. I'm boring. I even sound boring to myself."

"See, to some men that would just make you more

interesting, not less." He quirked an eyebrow. "Men like me, that is. It means you don't take as long as other women to get ready for a date and you might have more to talk about than gossip."

"You mean you don't care if a woman wears makeup?" she teased. "Or whether her dress is the latest style?"

He shook his head. "I think women worry about that kind of stuff way more than men do. I wouldn't want to have to wear all that junk that women buy by the cartful. Why would I care if you didn't either?"

She poked fun at the idea of him in a dress and heels. Aaron had a way about him that put a person right at ease. It was a gift, one she wished she had.

When she turned to say goodnight, she paused. At the intent look in his eyes, she realized he was about to kiss her. *Yes, please.* She met him halfway, reaching up to run her the fingers on her good hand through the hair on his neck as his lips met hers. She could feel strength, sure, but tenderness, too, as he sampled her lips. Taking a step closer, he gathered her in his arms and deepened it just enough for her toes to curl with pleasure inside her boots. When he pulled away, a knowing smile made his lips curve. "How about we hit Pete's after work tomorrow night? Burgers and beer—no makeup or dresses required."

"Sounds great." Her breathy voice sounded as if it belonged to another, sexier, woman. It didn't matter. He seemed to think she was sexy enough.

He tucked a few stray hairs behind her ears. "Six thirty work for you?"

"Six thirty, it is. Just call and let me know if you're running late so I don't worry."

"Will do." He waited as she went inside and locked the door, then she heard his thudding steps move downhill. Nerves had her puffing out a breath. She couldn't remember how long it had been since she had a date, but it was a lot longer since she'd had a decent one. No matter what happened, she knew they would have fun, and that was all she needed to know for now.

**** 

Aaron lay in his lonely bed for a long time, restless and unable to sleep. He hadn't felt a special bond with any woman in a long time, but he had with Harper from the very beginning. It wasn't just her looks that appealed to him, but her creative mind and her sense of humor. The fact that she embraced country life, like he did, was another positive to add to the growing list of her attributes. He felt as if there were strong possibilities for a close relationship here, connections he looked forward to investigating. At least in his experience, the chemistry between them was rare. And tonight, he felt her interest in their kiss which pleased him no end. He'd made good choices and bad choices when it came to women, like any other man, but it was clear which group she fell into. He'd put her, happily, at the top of his list. With that pleasurable thought in mind, he finally drifted off to sleep.

Work at the firehouse remained quiet the next day, a rare blessing. His men caught up on cleaning and repairing the large array of equipment along with mopping up the floors and cleaning the bathrooms. The latter was no one's favorite job, but the men did it without much complaint. He ran a tight ship, so if it stayed quiet, they'd run drills tomorrow to make sure everyone stayed in shape and at the top of their game.

The endless stack of paperwork kept him busy and he remembered that he needed to hire another man soon. They'd been one down for a few months now. At the stroke of six o'clock, he made his exit, looking forward to his date with Harper.

Back at home, he grabbed a quick shower and dressed in clean, pressed jeans, a checked shirt, and his best hat. It was a familiar look the locals jokingly called Texas formal. After one last check in the mirror, he exited, locking the house behind him. When he headed up the slope, Harper opened her door and met him on the porch. She wore the female version of his clothes, minus the hat, and it made a welcoming sight. "You look nice," he said with a smile. "I hope you're hungry."

"I'm starving. Don't be surprised if I out-eat you tonight."

Raising his eyebrows, he said, "I doubt that's possible, but feel free to astonish me." He clasped her hand in his as they walked to the truck, thankful she didn't pull away. Opening her door, he waited until she was belted to close it behind her. After he hopped in and started the engine, he said, "Tell me about your day."

'I got a lot done, actually. I finished building that coffee table I told you about with the old metal heating grates as the accent. It turned out even better than I hoped."

"You're not overdoing it by using your bad arm, are you? You don't want to screw up that cast and have to get it redone."

"No. I pretty much did the work one-handed, I promise. And most of the pieces were already cut. I just used the fingers of the other to steady things."

"Good. Did you get the glass you wanted to put on

41

the top? If not, we can run over tomorrow and get it."

"No need. Henry delivered it on his way to work. He cut it for me himself and it fits perfectly." The old man at the hardware store had glass cutting down to an art. "He even insisted on putting it in place to help me out. He's such a sweetie."

The gruff old devil was only sweet to her as far as he could tell, but he didn't correct her impression. Her positive attitude seemed to bring out the best in almost everyone she encountered. "That was kind of him. Can I get first dibs on that table? I really liked the components you made it with, so I know I'll love the finished product."

She'd been in his house, once, while he was getting changed and now, she called him on it. "Aaron, you know you already have a perfectly good coffee table."

"I've had that battered ol' thing since training. I bought it at a garage sale, because money was tight and I knew it would work for a while. I've been keeping an eye out for something I really like to replace it." He smiled at the dubious expression on her face. "Seriously. I upgrade certain things as I find pieces I'm interested in. That's one of the last items I need for now. I bet the one you made is just my style."

"Well, of course you can check it out and see if it fits your needs. You can even give it a trial run for a while if you want to be sure. But if you decide to keep it, I want to give it to you as a thank you gift."

"That's not happening." His jaw firmed. "I'll pay your usual price like everyone else."

"But—"

"I'll know if it's right when I see it in place. Pretty sure it'll be perfect. Enough said." He ignored her scowl and changed the subject. "What will you work on next?"

Recognizing the stubbornness she often saw in herself, she gave up. "I'm making a bar cart out of these vintage wooden boxes I found. Since I'm a little limited on maneuvering things right now, I might need a hand welding the metal foundation together. Handling that might be a little too much in my current state." She could see how to build it already in her head and it would be amazing.

"No problem. Just let me know when you need me to help." He turned a corner, heading along a side street that led onto the main drag. "What style would you call most of your creations, anyway? I don't know much about designing furniture."

"Most men would be hard pressed to know unless they're in the business. I'd say it's a mix between rustic and modern with industrial accents thrown in. I love old wood and metal. I do other styles of course, but that particular combination is my favorite."

"And you sell most of your items online?"

"About eighty percent. I'm fast friends with the post office and delivery service staff, because I'm always hauling sale items into both places." She grinned. "I also sell things at the flea market once a month. Those are mostly the less expensive items, like small furniture pieces and accessories. They sell really well there."

"I've never ventured over there to investigate. I guess I'm overdue."

"You're missing out. I've been going to flea markets for years and I really enjoy it. It's like a big treasure hunt. Pretty much everything is reasonably priced, too."

"I should give it a try."

"It's my favorite thing to do. I sell in the mornings

and early afternoons, then I close up and see if I can unearth a few bargains to drag home with me. And believe me, I always find something."

"So, you like dusty, decrepit things. No wonder you like me." He pulled into the restaurant lot and easily found a well-lit parking space, relishing her laughter. Turning the engine off, he glanced in her direction, raising his eyebrows. "We might get a thirty second reprieve before tongues start wagging. Ready to get the gossip buzz going?"

"There's no getting around it. Might as well get all the whispers back and forth over with." She met him on the pavement, leaving him to shut and lock the door behind her. Shepherding her in front of him, he opened the heavy glass door, let her in and followed her into the entry. Soft country music crooned in the background. They waited while the busy hostess sat a previous couple. The glances that zipped their way immediately inspired laughter which they managed to stifle. A few people even looked shocked with their gaping mouths giving them away. What should have been solely their business would spread through town like rushing water flowing downhill. Everyone in town would know in the morning that the fire chief was dating Harper Lindsey and that was just fine with him. He couldn't have cared less what they thought. She would probably be quite shocked to know he'd happily stick a brand on her any way he could, like any good Texan. He wouldn't pressure her, but he had no problem striking a claim before anyone else could find a way to finagle a spot beside her.

The welcoming hostess led them to a cozy booth at the back of the room where they'd be surrounded by less noise and have some privacy. Harper didn't have to know he'd called in a favor to get that rare privilege. The back booths were considered a worthy prize frequently fought over, especially on the weekends. Numerous people greeted them or waved a hello on the way past. She agreed to let him sit in the gunslinger's position with his back against the wall so he could see anyone approach. Protective habits die hard. The slab of wood that served as a table wasn't overly large, but big enough for two to be comfortable. Red, cushioned bench seats had just been re-stuffed or so he'd heard. Taking off his hat, he laid it beside him. "I like your hat," she said. "Some men look ridiculous in them, like they watched too many westerns growing up. Yours looks like it was made for you."

Crossing his arms on the table, he grinned. "Funny you should say that. It was, actually. My mother's a professional hat maker."

"Are you joking? I always thought they were machine-made."

"Most are, but not in this case. The skill was passed down from her father and when her brothers weren't interested, she decided to give it a try."

"Good for her."

"She's got a terrific reputation now with more online business than she can handle. And I'm lucky I didn't have to pay for mine, because she charges a fortune. A lot of people think a custom fit is worth the extra cost." As always, when he thought of his mother, he felt a swell of pride.

"That's really interesting. I'd love to watch her work sometime. I bet it's fascinating."

They were both creative women and he hoped it

would give them something to talk about when they met. "Sure. If you behave yourself, I'll get her to make one for you."

She grimaced. "I look like a total dork in hats. Like some goofy kid playing dress-up with a grownup's clothes. And that's a drag, because I love them."

"Don't worry. Mom will hunt down just the right style for you. She's been doing it for years and she's got a magic touch."

"You two sound like you're close."

"Yup. I'm a momma's boy from way back and proud of it." He handed her one of the red, plastic-coated menus and checked his out. His only question was what version of a burger he wanted tonight. He'd tried and enjoyed them all. After a moment, his eyes met hers over the top. "There's only one rule. You're not allowed to tease me about how much I eat."

"I wouldn't dare. I told you I was starving, so it's all fair game tonight."

"Good. And we're going to have dessert, too, so save enough room. I can't leave without having at least one piece of Sally's rhubarb pie." All of the sweets were supplied by the local bakery and the sugary delights just flew off the shelf. The baker's business had tripled when the restaurant started carrying her goods. Thanks to them, his pants were a little tighter than they used to be.

Ty and Sandra's daughter, Mindy, worked here two nights a week. She brought them each a beer, then stood and giggled with them for a moment before she had to scurry away. She was a hard worker, just like her parents. When she came back a few minutes later, they ordered bacon cheeseburgers and onion rings. Thank goodness, there were three different sizes of burgers. Harper got a medium and he ordered two larges. That was one major benefit of having a physical job with a weight room on site; he and the other men stayed pretty fit no matter what they ate.

Mid-conversation, he watched as one of the young, local women headed their way and he sighed. Stacy Metters had put the moves on him more times than he could count, ignoring the unwelcome fact that he had not only never encouraged her efforts, but had actively discouraged them. She was the very opposite of his type and her persistence wore his legendary patience thin. Sashaying to his side of the table, she turned to smirk at Harper, tossing her faux ebony curls over one shoulder. "Well, what a surprise. I sure didn't expect to see you two here together." Her words were said through clenched teeth framed by a smile so fake it tickled him.

He struggled to be polite. "Oh, and why is that, Stacy?"

"It gave me a laugh, to be honest. Isn't she a little young for you?" She tapped a glittering fingernail on the table. "Aren't you just outta high school, hon?"

Pink bloomed on Harper's cheeks, but she managed a grin. "You're about sixteen years behind the times, but thanks for the compliment." Her easy sense of humor delighted him, but didn't please Stacy, judging by the pinched look on her face.

"Have you met Harper, Stacy?"

"More or less. I know who she is." Stacy's nose wrinkled and she pouted, her enhanced lips looking like a rabid squirrel had bitten her. "Well, once you tuck her in and read her a bedtime story, come find me. I'm sure we can think of something interesting to do. Maybe set a little fire of our own." She gave an audible purr and he

47

wondered how long she'd practiced it in the mirror.

Every fireman he knew had heard that tired old line one too many times. "I think I'll pass, but nice to see you. You run along and have a good night, now." For a moment, she just stared at him in disbelief. Then, with a dramatic whirl, she stomped away, putting her high heels at risk of snapping off. He couldn't stifle an exasperated groan, struggling not to add an adolescent eye roll.

Harper raised an eyebrow. "Let me guess. This isn't the first time she's made a rather over-the-top play for you."

"Not the first by a long shot, I'm afraid. Sorry about that. She can be hard to get rid of and I've given up trying to be tactful about it."

She watched as the other woman settled back into her seat, leaning to whisper into one of her friend's ears. "I guess she's sort of pretty if you don't mind the extra enhancements."

"I prefer a woman with a more natural look, myself." He tapped her hand with one finger. "Present company definitely included." They sat back so Mindy could deliver their meals. The servings were plentiful and the tempting aroma made his stomach grumble in anticipation. Taking all the items off the tray, they handed it back to Mindy so they'd have enough room on the table to be comfortable. They dug in and ate in companionable silence. He smiled when she started to slow down before finishing her burger. "Lightweight," he teased after he dug into his second portion with gusto. She nibbled at her cooling onion rings as he continued chowing down. When he finally finished, he sat back with a happy groan. "Now, that's a perfect meal."

"Want the rest of my rings?"

"Better not, thanks. Gotta leave a little room for that pie."

"Oh, seriously?" she groaned. "How could you possibly have any room left? These burgers are always so filling."

"I warned you. It's not a night out without dessert." He laughed at the incredulous expression on her face. "C'mon, girl, it's the best pie in the state. If you miss out, you'll live to regret it."

"What is it about men and their love of pie?"

He peered at her, his head cocked to one side. "You'd order something chocolate, wouldn't you?"

"Of course. As far as I'm concerned, those are the only calories you never regret."

"Well, what is it about women and chocolate?"

She wiggled her eyebrows at him, smirking. "Some say it's better than sex."

"Well, then, dang, they're doin' it wrong." She burst out laughing, causing a few nearby folks to turn their way and smile. Aaron cherished the happy sound. After all that she'd been through, she could still laugh. He admired her resilient attitude.

Mindy came to check on them. "Ready for dessert, you two?"

"None for me." Harper rubbed her stomach. "I'm stuffed. But I think he wants some pie."

"You're not getting away that easily," he said. "Mindy, why don't you box up a piece of rhubarb pie and a slice of that chocolate mousse cake for us. We'll take them home and eat them later." Smiling, she hurried away to package them.

Harper tsk tsked, shaking her head. "Such a bad influence. You're going to make me gain weight and I don't need any encouragement in that department."

"Women worry way too much about what the scale says. I never get on one. I just adjust if my jeans get too tight." He liked some curves to cuddle and, hopefully, he'd soon get a chance to do exactly that. In a few minutes, Mindy returned with their package. He paid the bill. They stood to leave, him carrying the package in one hand and holding her hand with the other. A few people's eyes followed them out, Stacy's burning a hole in his back as they crossed to the door.

Chapter Five

Outside, the air had cooled to a night chill. Aaron put a warming arm around Harper's shoulders and saw her into the truck, setting the sweets down on the rubber mat by her feet. Once inside, he started the truck and turned on the heat. "It's cooler than the weatherman predicted tonight."

She giggled. When he raised his eyebrows in question, she said, "I was just thinking about your lovelorn admirer. I should feel sorry for Stacy, getting turned down by you, but she's always been such a witch to me."

He snorted. "Add the letter $B$ to that word instead of a $W$ and you'd be about right."

Now, she busted into full-on laughter. "Shame on you. I was trying to be tactful."

He started on their drive home. "Why waste your time? No, predatory women like that are a huge turnoff, at least to me. She bought half her body at the surgeon's office and the other half at the makeup counter." He smiled. "Like I said earlier, I prefer a natural woman. That way, you really know what you're getting. No man wants half of the woman who attracts you to end up back in the bathroom drawer." Impossible to see if Harper was blushing, but he'd bet his paycheck on it.

"I don't think she has many problems getting a date. She brags about that all of the time to anyone who'll listen."

"More like a one-night stand, maybe. I don't see many men foolish enough to ask for a repeat performance. Her constant need for attention is exhausting."

Her voice took on a teasing tone. "Don't act too innocent, now. I'd lay a bet that you've had a few of those ladies in your life. And I doubt you turned them all away."

"Not since I was young and stupid. I learned, eventually, what type of woman really interested me and what didn't." He glanced at her. "You forget I'm an old man compared to you."

"Six years isn't much of a difference. Not to me, anyway."

So, she'd been motivated enough to find out his age before now. *Good*. And the difference didn't seem to bother her. It surprised him how much her interest meant to him. "Well, it makes me happy that you feel that way, at least." After another few minutes, he turned into his darkened driveway and started up the lane. "Want to pull some chairs up next to the fire pit and relax?"

"Sure, for a while anyway. I think we both know I won't last too long on a full stomach." They left the truck and wandered to the back lawn. Getting her settled, he put the fire together. After a while, he mentioned that his mother and sister lived nearby. "Oh, that's so nice. Are you close?"

"Yeah, we hang out once every week or two. Usually, we have a meal to catch up on whatever's going on in our lives." He paused, not wanting to be insensitive. "How old were you when your mom died?"

"Eight. Sometimes, it seems like yesterday. I still

think about her every day."

Aaron understood. He felt the same way about his father. "And who did you live with afterward?"

"You know the children's home on the other side of Springvale?"

"Yes. The one that looks like a school, right?"

She nodded. "I lived there until I was eighteen."

He should have realized. She'd never spoken about any other family members. "No one adopted you?" Realizing how rude that sounded, he apologized.

She waved his concern away. "Don't be silly. That's a reasonable question." Sighing, she continued. "I had problems that most people didn't want to deal with. Being abandoned by parents, twice, in different ways, gave me nightmares and other issues. I didn't make friends easily." Meeting his gaze, she said, "It was fine. You always hear horror stories about places like that, but the staff members always treated me well. I think they felt sorry for me. By the time I was eighteen, I was well-prepared to take care of myself."

It bothered him to think that no one had cared enough to give her a family. "You must be incredibly proud of yourself. You survived a lot of heartbreak at such a young age."

"Sometimes I'm proud, but other times, I just feel different from everyone else." She shrugged. "Depends on the day, I guess, like anybody else. I miss both of them, but my mother, especially, because I don't have much to remember her by."

"I'm serious about how strong you are. A lot of people would feel like a victim, but you're one of the most positive people I know."

"Thanks. That's a sweet thing to say." It was great

to see her smile again. To lighten things up, he told her a few funny stories about his family before walking her up to the cabin.

He thought about her for a long time after he returned to the house. It would be hard to imagine his life without his parents and sister. They had all been healthy and happy until his father died. Still, his mother and sister carried on with their productive lives. Both had careers and, although his mother said she'd never remarry, she had a lot of friends she enjoyed spending time with. They'd all been close growing up and it wasn't until he got older that he realized just how lucky he was to have them.

As he sat mulling things over, Ty called. "I thought I'd let you know that Harper checked out squeaky clean. Can't say I'm surprised, but at least we covered the basics. Even the folks at the children's home said she was a lovely girl, a little quiet, but well-liked by everyone."

"That doesn't surprise me."

"No, but it's good to check something off our list, isn't it?" He stifled a chuckle. "Heard the two of you had a date at Pete's."

"Word travels fast."

"Mindy said she's a sweetie pie—her words, not mine."

He smiled, enjoying the contentedness the idea brought. "Your daughter's pretty smart. I couldn't put it any better myself."

\*\*\*\*

In the nearby town of Springvale, the arsonist inspected the old, dilapidated shed, a full gas can in hand. The abandoned building was bursting with rotting, termite-ridden wood, stuffed garbage bags, and cobwebs, just as he expected. *How convenient.* You couldn't ask for better kindling. His worn hiking boots were wrapped with bubble wrap and secured with heavy tape to blur his footprints. As always in these situations, he wore gloves. He was no amateur, not with all his past experience. In a very real sense, fire had become his only friend. An old friend, at that, the very best kind. Setting fires offered an almost biblical healing he couldn't find anywhere else.

Tonight, since he couldn't figure out yet how to get access to Harper, he would settle for the sacrifice of this building. The climbing flames would warm and heal him. Fire fed him the way heroin and whisky soothed others, but to call it an addiction would demean it. It was the very definition of power, not weakness. The resulting calm afterward would allow him the patience to come up with a plan guaranteed to defeat his nemesis. Puzzling over the various details of tonight's entertainment, he decided to leave just one large puddle of gasoline in the center and set fire to the refuse closest to the walls. That way, he could watch the shed burn for a little longer than normal before he had to leave for his own safety. He just didn't want his fix to be over too soon.

The closest house on this quiet county road was out of sight, over a sloping, grassy hill. Even if vigilant inhabitants caught sight of the trails of smoke, they would call the local firehouse, which was a good twenty minutes away. Those wailing sirens always gave him plenty of time to flee. The fire chief in this town was an inept fool, part of the reason this area had become his own favorite playing ground rather than his hometown. The moron in charge would never connect it to the fire at Harper's place. He wouldn't care enough to try. All he focused on was the many ways to pad his paycheck and whether his newest bottle of scotch was within reach.

Twisting the cover off the red plastic container, he poured the potent liquid out slowly, making a winding pattern on the refuse as any true artist would. He watched as all the deadly tributaries joined in the center to make a small pool. Satisfied the area was drenched, he carried the can to the exterior to prevent an accident. On his return, he stood by the battered door. Wrapping a stone inside a piece of refuse to weigh it down, he lit the edges of the paper with his lighter and threw it onto the piles two feet away. The burn started slowly, nibbling like a child with a chocolate bar as it first melted a garbage bag close by. As it gained momentum, he felt pleasure spread through his body, almost sexual in its intensity. His pulse sped up and his muscles tightened. As the flames finally crept to the center, they met the waiting gasoline and those flames leapt in ecstasy toward the ceiling, the resulting sound a familiar, intoxicating pulse. The inferno that followed was a work of art with him as its creator. As the roof joined in with the chaos, he moved reluctantly away. Now that the growing fire was intense enough, he threw the gas can on top as his parting gesture, watching as it melted.

Satisfied with the night's sacrifice, he took one last, lingering look and began the short hike up the hill to the tree line. He would enjoy a two-mile hike through the deep woods to where he'd parked his car, tucked away off another county road. Once he was well clear of the site, he would take his boots off, don the sneakers hidden in his backpack, and run the rest of the way. Rampant pleasure filled his soul and gave him more than enough energy to power his escape.

## Chapter Six

After breakfast the next morning, Aaron and Harper were in the barn, working on her bar cart. They heard the growling sound of a vehicle approaching and he leaned out to see who might be coming to call. Ty and Sandra pulled up the driveway in their truck and parked. Stepping out, he shaded his eyes until he saw them exiting the vehicle, and waved them over. "What are you guys up to this morning?"

They were dressed in matching jeans and cotton shirts, the vision of a country couple, which made him smile. Ty stepped up and shook his hand. "We were running some errands and took a chance you'd be at home. Can I have a word? I thought the girls could talk inside." That was code for "let's have a private chat." As Sandra entered the barn, they strolled down the dusty lane, closer to the house.

Ty wouldn't drop in without calling first unless it was important. Aaron paused by the deck, leaning against the thick, wooden rail. "What's up?"

"Did you hear Springvale had a fire last night, around midnight? One of my deputies was in the area and gave me a heads up."

"I hadn't heard. Chief Johnson and I aren't exactly close."

Ty rolled his eyes. "He's a disgrace. I wish they'd replace him." Sighing, he continued. "Anyway, I've been keeping an ear out for any incidences of fires using gasoline as an accelerant. Because I wondered if maybe Harper's fire could be connected to others. Maybe he doesn't just concentrate on one area."

"That's possible. Did you call Johnson and ask him for any details?"

"I didn't waste my breath, but the assistant chief was far more accommodating. Rocky Ransom's only twenty-eight, but he's got a good head on his shoulders. When I called their firehouse this morning, I spoke to him and he confirmed it was set with gasoline."

"Was it a house or what?"

"Just an old shed, but a decent size one. By the time Johnson got his butt there with his men, the shed was gone along with half the pasture. Luckily, there are no neighbors nearby." He paused. "Do you want to run over with me and take a look? It's his day off, but Rocky said he'd be willing to meet us there."

"Sure. Having a look around can't hurt." It might be stretching credibility a bit that it was the same offender, but he couldn't deny that Ty had an almost uncanny instinct about such things. They also had no other leads to pursue. "Let me tell Harper what we're doing."

"Sure. She and Sandra can just hang out until we get back. It won't take that long."

They were seated in his truck and on the road within ten minutes. The drive would take another twenty. Ty texted Rocky, who said he still hadn't been able to reach his chief, but he'd meet them there, as promised. On the drive over, Aaron told Ty about Stacy's behavior at the diner the previous night and the other man laughed. "Some things never change," he mused. "Stacy never did like to hear the word 'no.' She used to show up on my doorstep when I was single, peddling her wares. And if you ever tell Sandra that, I'll shoot you myself." He shook his head. "She's got a jealous streak."

"Don't worry. Your secret's safe with me."

"I didn't realize you were interested in Harper until she told me you'd asked her out."

Ty was his best friend and he told him almost everything. He sighed. "Who wants to admit they were rejected, even nicely?"

"It's strange, isn't it? Probably the first time a fire turned things in your favor."

"That's true. I don't think trusting people is very easy for her. She doesn't have anyone around to protect her if anything goes wrong."

"Maybe that was true before, but she has all of us now."

"That's true and I'm glad for her."

Finding the correct location with the help of GPS, they turned off the county road into a ravaged field. They drove up the barely visible track to the charred remains of the building and stopped to park a short distance away. The blackened earth split out in a sunburst pattern around the scant remains of the shed. Most of the field had charred to a crisp, only strips of gold and green for relief. One other truck was parked nearby, a tall, stocky man leaning against its back bumper. The younger guy waiting sucked a drink from a to-go cup, his blond hair shining under the sunlight. After they parked, Ty climbed out first. "Hey, Rocky. I don't think you've met Aaron Lassiter. He's our fire chief."

"Chief." He stepped forward to shake his hand. "A pleasure to meet you. I'm not sure if your fire and mine are linked, but you're free to have a look. I'll tell you what little I know."

"Thanks, Appreciate it. I assume you couldn't reach your boss?"

"No, sir. He's still not answering. I apologize for that."

"Oh, well. It's not your fault. Thanks for meeting us, especially when I know it's your day off." He let the two other men stroll around to have a look while he leaned down and peered at the shapes the assistant chief had flagged that led away from the fire. They had an indistinct outline which made them absolutely no help. "These the tracks you mentioned to Ty?"

The younger man moved closer. "Yes, sir. They looked strange to me, but they're the only ones I found."

Nodding, he straightened. "Yup, those are his tracks. He covered his boots with something to ensure we couldn't get a clear print. Suspects don't know to obscure evidence like that if it's their first time." He felt a frisson of excitement run down his back. "This could be our guy. How far do the tracks lead?"

"Almost half a mile. Then they trail farther into the woods, off the path, and disappear into the brush." He frowned. "I was going to try and track them today. I didn't have enough men or light last night and my chief thought it was a waste of time."

Johnson probably thought any job was more effort than should be required. The three of them decided to follow the prints with the idea that the more eyes on the lookout, the better. They trailed the marks under the spreading canopy of trees until they disappeared into the deepest part of the woods. Pausing, Aaron said, "He wore the camouflaged footwear until it was safe to slide into the dense forest, where he wouldn't leave any tracks.

So, he either parked farther away or he lives close enough to walk back. I would bet on the former. What do you two think?"

The other two men agreed. The forest floor was covered with too many rotting leaves and fallen branches to hold any prints, so they returned to the original site. Rocky pivoted to face Aaron. "Do you think we should have a look at all of the small fires that have taken place in this entire area?"

It was exactly what he and Ty had been thinking, so the younger man's initiative impressed him. "Yes, I think that's our next step." He peered at him, considering. "Who trained you?" He recognized the man's name Rocky provided as one of the best instructors in the state. "And how do you like working under Chief Johnson?" Any blind man could see the younger man was struggling for a tactful answer, so he waited, trying not to grin.

Rocky clutched his hat in his hands. "I'm happy to have the job, but, in all honesty, I wish I was in a position where I could learn more. Chief Johnson is happy to keep his underlings at a standstill if you get what I mean." He gave a sheepish smile. "I'd prefer you didn't let my opinion get back to him, though. I need the paycheck."

"We'll keep it between the three of us. No worries." He trusted his instincts. "Our department's a man short. I haven't advertised because I prefer to hand pick my men. If you're interested in applying, we can keep it between us." The keen light in the other man's eyes made him chuckle. "Come see me on your next day off and we'll talk." Taking the young man's phone, he plugged in his number.

"I can't tell you how grateful I am, Chief, for even a

chance to be on your team."

"You're welcome." They had another look around the ravaged site, finding the point of origin, but everything else that might have yielded further information was lost. Saying goodbye to their new friend, they made their way home.

On the way, Ty chewed a piece of gum, a thoughtful look on his face. "I don't know what we'll find, but, you're right. We have to at least try to determine if there's a connection between the two fires. Because, if there is, there may be more we're not aware of."

"Finding similar fires would make sense, right? We know he couldn't have such a long stretch between fires even if his primary goal was always Harper. But if he had smaller fires that satisfied him for a reasonable length of time, that might be enough to keep his desires under control."

"Why use fire? Why not kill her another way if he wanted her dead?"

"Arsonists are a different breed. Some just like to destroy buildings for the hell of it. Just one more form of simple vandalism. For others, it's just another kind of murder." Aaron shrugged. "Psychologically, it's almost like fire is both their religion and their drug. Who knows, it might even have some kind of religious significance to him."

"But what could a young woman like Harper have done to cause such explosive hatred?"

"That's the question of the hour, isn't it?" After a moment, he said, "The interesting thing is that it's not just us that have no idea. She doesn't, either. So, the motive's either something dead simple that she'd never bother to think about or something offbeat, some insignificant slight that only means something to the arsonist."

"That makes sense to me."

As they approached his place, they decided to put any further discussion on hold, not wanting to upset the other two. Parking in front of the barn, they found the women looking at Harper's treasures. Sandra greeted them with a grin. "I just tried to buy your coffee table. It's gorgeous."

"No way, lady. I have first dibs," he teased. "If you behave yourself, maybe she can build you something similar." After a few minutes, she left with Ty, along with a promise that Harper would build her a table with a similar look she'd love.

After grabbing a tasty bite of lunch, they returned to hang out in the barn, happy to get out of the blazing heat of the direct sun. While she stained a book shelf, transforming the piece with a few simple strokes, he poked around. After a while, he noticed a large, intricate wooden box that looked out of place sitting on top of the stack of rough lumber. About twelve inches square and quite deep, it had intricate carving that covered the top and sides. "What's this?"

She glanced up and paused. "After the fire, it's the only thing I have left of my mother's. If I hadn't been getting ready to repair the hinge, it wouldn't have been in the shed. A small, silver lining to the fire, I guess, because it has a few papers and photos of hers in it."

"The workmanship is beautiful. Do you know where it originally came from?"

"Spain, I think. Her parents were affluent and she spent a semester there in college." She put her brush down. "There are a few pictures of her inside, thank goodness. Otherwise, I'd have nothing to remember her by."

"Can I take a peek? I'll be careful."

"Sure."

He opened the lid and found two photographs lying on top of some old papers. One was of a striking woman holding a baby. Peering in her face, he saw a strong resemblance to Harper. The other photograph was one of her mother posing in a lush garden, huge sunflowers brushing her shoulders. The woman was stunning and grinning from ear-to-ear as she held some colorful blooms. "Your mother was beautiful."

"Thanks. I always thought so. She was a very loving mom. I still miss her."

"And your dad?"

She stilled, and seeing her jaw tense, he wished he hadn't asked. "My dad left when I was four. We never heard from him again."

"I'm sorry, Harper. I didn't mean to bring up unhappy memories."

"Don't worry, it's fine." She shrugged. "It's a shame that I don't remember much about him. Whenever I'd get mad about it, she'd just say the end of their marriage was more her fault than his. I figured she was making excuses for him."

"He missed out on a fabulous daughter. His loss and probably his biggest regret."

"That's a kind thing to say. How about your dad?"

His dad's death still saddened him and he felt the usual tug of pain. "He suffered a fatal heart attack ten years ago. Never made it to the hospital. He died in my mother's arms."

"Now, I'm the one who's sorry." She leaned over to

stroke his arm. "Were the two of you close?"

"Very." He smiled, feeling a little guilty that his situation was far less dramatic than hers. "I couldn't have had better parents if I custom-ordered them. He taught me everything I know about being an honorable man."

"Well, I know I would have liked him, then, because you're the best man I know. He'd be so proud of you."

He felt a flush of pleasure at her words. She wasn't one to give empty compliments. "Thanks. That means a lot."

"Your mom never re-married?"

Shaking his head, he answered, "She always said she did it right the first time. Why should she settle for second best the second time around?"

"That's so romantic. And I would have to agree. Sometimes, your first love really is your last."

"My father would say that stuff is a lot of nonsense, but he still brought her flowers all the time. He'd say, 'Bought some posies for the prettiest girl in town.' " Aaron wasn't sure why he'd added that last, private thought. She was so easy to talk to, but he felt bad when he spied the tears leaking from her eyes and changed the subject.

Chapter Seven

The next morning, Aaron was surprised to find Rocky waiting for him when he arrived at the firehouse. He bid him good morning, noting he was lacking the warm smile he'd worn yesterday. Something had happened. "I know you weren't expecting me today," he blurted out, shifting from one foot to the other. "I was wondering if you could spare me a few minutes of your time."

He saw the other men eyeing him with curiosity and waved him into his office. "Of course. Sorry you had to wait. Are you here about the job?"

"Yes, sir." He sighed and fumbled with the baseball cap in his hands. "I think it's only fair that I tell you I got fired yesterday."

He looked at him, shocked to the core. Now, that he wasn't expecting. From the calls he'd made about this guy after they'd talked and the enthusiastic endorsement he'd received, he would expect every staff member to get fired before him. "What the hell for?"

"Chief lost his mind when he found out you'd been looking at his fire site. Said I shouldn't have allowed you access. He didn't seem to care that he wasn't answering his phone so I could ask permission." Shuffling his feet, he admitted, "I'll be honest with you, his reaction really threw me for a loop. I didn't sleep an hour last night. I've never been fired from anywhere in my entire life."

He felt a stab of regret. "I feel terrible that I put you in this position. I've never had a fellow fire chief act that territorial about his district before today. It didn't occur to me that simply taking a look would be a problem."

"Me, either. I'm a little puzzled about it, to tell you the truth. He's always grouchy, but I've never seen him blow a gasket like that." He shrugged. "Why would he care if another fire chief took a look around? It doesn't make any sense."

*Because he's a lazy bully, but that's a problem for another day.* "Well, maybe things happen for a reason." He dragged a few papers from the corner of his desk. "After our visit, I talked with your head instructor and a few others you've worked alongside. They were all very complimentary about your skills, your work ethic and your attitude."

"That's wonderful to hear, especially after the day I had yesterday."

"I imagine so. Think of it this way, though. He might have made this transfer little easier." He passed him the papers in his hand. "Why don't you take a seat and read through the salary information and benefits package?"

"Thanks. That sounds great."

He caught up on paperwork while the younger man sat and checked out all of the provided information. When he raised his head after reading the last page, Aaron said, "What do you think? Would you be satisfied with those terms?"

"Yes, sir. It's a little more than I was getting paid before and the benefits will work for me." He grinned. "Does that mean I have the job?"

"Yes, it does. I'll expect you to work hard, like everyone else. In return, I'll try to expand your education while we work. Sound fair?"

"It sure does. When should I start?"

"Do you need to work out any days before you leave Johnson's department?"

"No, sir. His exact words were, Get the hell out. I don't want to see your butt-kissin' face around here ever again. And, even if he changes his mind, I have enough owed vacation to cover, anyway."

That bit of information certainly simplified things. "Well, that's clear enough. Want to start tomorrow morning?"

He grinned. "Yes, sir."

"And call me Aaron when it's just us. In public, just Chief is fine."

"Thank you, Aaron."

"You're welcome. Make sure you get a decent night's sleep and I'll see you in the morning. Eight o'clock sharp—don't be late." He watched him stride out of the office, a different man than the one who'd come in just moments ago. If Rocky worked hard and kept his great attitude, he and the rest of the team would get along just fine.

The next morning, Aaron arrived at work a little early just to see if his intuition proved correct. Sure enough, Rocky was already standing beside the engines, introducing himself to the men. "Good morning," he said with a grin. "I wanted to get a running start. Hope that's okay."

"Extra initiative is always appreciated here." He waved for him to follow. "The first couple of days, I want you to stick close to Jim. He's my senior officer. He'll show you how we do things around here."

"Great."

"My assistant, Cherie, will take care of your photo identification first thing. You'll find a locker and bed with your name on it, so you can settle in. After that, Jim will put you to work. Any questions so far?"

"No, Chief. I wanted to tell you one thing, though." He grimaced. "One of the guys called to warn me that Chief Johnson is on the warpath. Apparently, he thought he was just teaching me a lesson and planned to hire me back at a lower rate when I came crawling back as he put it."

"Oh, he did, did he? Well, don't worry about that. I'll take care of him. Just do your job."

"Yes, I will. Thanks." He watched as the young man joined Jim and they walked away together. He had high hopes for Rocky. He'd have to wait and see if they panned out.

Lunch was over and the men were out on a routine call when Chief Johnson came calling. Thanks to his total lack of decent manners, there was no warning before Aaron's office door was thrown open, to bang on the inside wall. He glanced up, settling against the back of his desk chair. "Well, Ira, it's been a while. What can I do for you?"

The other man frowned, his face puckering as if he'd swallowed sour milk. He hitched up his pants under an oversize, sagging belly. "You wanna tell me why the hell you're poaching my men? We don't do that kind of thing around here. You're outta line."

Nothing like turning the situation around to suit your own needs. "The only employee I have on my team who came from your department was fired yesterday. I simply hired him immediately afterward. You have no grounds for filing a complaint." The firing had actually done him

70

a favor by simplifying Rocky's transition to his new department.

He bared his teeth like a junkyard dog, exposing the yellow-tinged evidence of a heavy smoker. The faint aroma of whisky drifted between them. "You got a lot of nerve. First you stick your uppity nose in where you don't belong and then you make a grab for my boy."

He'd never actually heard the word uppity used in real life and thought it was pretty funny to be called that under the circumstances. Smothering his distaste for the man, he spoke calmly. "Rocky tried to get ahold of you to get permission for us to have a look at your site. You weren't answering your phone, even after multiple attempts. We were just trying to ascertain whether your fire and mine are connected."

"I'm the boss of that station, not that little ass-kisser."

"Which is why we tried to contact you first. Perhaps if you made yourself available to your staff and other local chiefs, having us compare notes wouldn't have been an issue. This situation may have turned out differently."

He slapped a meaty fist down on Aaron's desk with a bang, scattering a pile of papers. "That's not how we do things in the country. You're just a transplanted city boy. You don't know to get along with our kind."

"I have no problems getting along with anyone else in the country. This is where I belong now. I doubt that it's a coincidence that the only person around here I don't get along with is you." Aaron stood to tower over the other man, stifling a smile as he took an unsteady step back. "You made a serious mistake firing Rocky. He's a good natured, hard-working, young man. I'm thrilled to have him and I'm sure he'll fit in here." He narrowed his eyes. "Maybe you should value your staff a little more."

"You arrogant asshole. You think you're in charge around here?" He took another step back and growled, "We'll just see about that." Whirling, he stormed out, pausing to kick the metal garbage can like a child in a tantrum, leaving the distinct aroma of body odor behind. The container spun and toppled over as the sound of his stomping boots retreated down the stairs. Aaron moved into the open hall to watch him depart, not trusting him to keep his grimy hands to himself. The man was a disgrace to their profession.

It made him wonder why he was quite so angry about him and Ty seeing the fire scene. Did he know more than he was saying? Or was he just angry about Rocky? It wasn't clear—only time would tell.

At the end of the day, he pulled Jim aside to ask him how Rocky had done with the day's work. The older man smiled, running a hand through his graying hair. "I think he's going to fit in great. He's sharp as a pencil, but easy to get along with, too. The others seemed to like him already."

"Good. That's what I was hoping." He told him about Johnson's surprise visit.

"That man's a moron. I can't believe he's kept his job this long. He should have been fired years ago." He shook his head, sighing. "Well, I'm cookin' tonight. You staying for dinner?"

"No, I think I'll head back to the house."

The other man raised his eyebrows and smiled. "That wouldn't have anything to do with a certain blonde, would it?"

"It just might." Jim walked away, heading for the

kitchen. Aaron called it a day and went home, glad the drive was a short one. On arrival, he found a scribbled note on his front door. It read, "I made supper tonight. Grab a shower if you like and come up. It's ready when you are."

In the shower, he thought about how domestic their situation had become and how comforting. Some men might find it boring, but he spent the whole day with people, sometimes grieving people, and it was so nice to come home to a smiling face. Especially when that face belonged to Harper. Being together felt natural and easier than any relationship he'd ever had with a woman. He felt so relaxed around her. That led to a surprising thought and he admitted the simple truth of it. If he could get her in his bed, then his life would be complete. An added benefit was that his mother might stop hinting about him settling down. She didn't nag as much as some others would, but she wasn't above a pointed hint about him still being a bachelor now and then.

He changed into fresh jeans and a shirt, not bothering with a jacket for the short walk up the hill. Scanning his surroundings as he walked, he realized the green leaves would soon be changing to an annual bounty of reds and yellows. Autumn being his favorite season, he looked forward to it. Harper swung the door open to his knock. "Perfect timing." She took his arm and led him into the kitchen. The smell of beef cooking in the oven made his stomach growl. "You'd better like cheeseburger casserole, or we're screwed."

"Most men like beef, especially here in Texas, so that's a pretty safe bet. Can't say I've tried that kind of casserole before, though, but it smells wonderful. And I'm starving."

"Well, the good news is, I may not be a fabulous cook, but I can prepare this just fine. It's one of my favorites." She gestured at the cluttered counter where empty packages and dirty spoons covered the surface. "All the ingredients go into one big baking dish, so it's easy to make, even one-handed, with not many dishes left to wash. Can you lift it out of the oven for me? I'll grab our plates off the table and serve."

He did as she asked, the aroma of tomatoes and melting cheese revving his appetite. Setting it on the surface of the stove, he took off the lid and stepped back, letting her take over. Using a big spoon, she filled his plate. Giving herself a portion about a third of the size. "That's not enough to keep you alive," he protested.

She laughed and the sound warmed him. "I'd grow as fat as one of Mr. Latham's hogs if I listened to you. While it's certainly not fair, women cannot eat nearly as much as men do."

"You're right. That doesn't seem fair." Sitting at the table, they dug in and he groaned with pleasure at the very first bite. "This is delicious. Where did you find the recipe?"

"On one of those online sites that specialize in one dish meals. I don't mind cooking, but I hate having a lot of clean-up to do afterward." She chatted about the work she'd completed that day in between bites while he ate and enjoyed listening. When he started to slow down eating, he told her about Rocky and the squabble with Chief Johnson. "He sounds like a jerk."

"Believe me, that's the nicest term I could possibly call him." With a sigh, he finished his last forkful. "That was delicious."

"Do you want some more? There's plenty left."

"That depends. Did I see cookies in there, too?"

"You nosy stinker." She gave an exaggerated pout. "I swear you've got some kind of native instinct about desserts. They were supposed to be a surprise."

He stood and picked up both their empty plates, carrying them to the sink to rinse before putting them in the dishwasher. "Baked goods never escape my highly tuned radar."

Putting a handful of the treats on a plate, she preceded him to the couch, setting them on the low table. "Do you want some coffee?"

"I'm all coffeed out. How about a big glass of milk if you've got it?"

Returning to the kitchen, she poured them both a serving and brought the glasses to set on the table while he grabbed the treats. He took a bite and rolled his eyes. "Hope you made extra. Two of these will last me about five minutes, then I'll be begging for more."

"Oh, I've already got your number. I made a dozen for you to take home for yourself and another two dozen for the guys at the firehouse. That should take care of everybody for now."

He felt oddly touched that she'd bothered going to all that extra work when she still didn't have full use of her arm. Especially when his share of the cookies would be guaranteed to disappear in a day or two. "If you're looking to win a popularity contest, that cinched your win. The guys are shameless. They'll do almost anything for a cookie."

"Good to know. If I need forgiveness for any mistakes in the future, I'll just bake."

****

While Aaron worked late at the station, Harper

gulped down a grilled chicken sandwich on her own and returned to work in the barn. The artificial light from above left dark corner pockets and shadows on the wall. It felt strange and a little spooky to be working in here without him. How paranoid was that? They'd both become used to their nightly routine of eating together and then hanging out. Sometimes, they puttered in the barn and others, just watched something on television. A simple life, one that she'd always hoped to share with someone special. It occurred to her that maybe she might be becoming a little too dependent on him for both company and security. For someone like her who was used to being alone, it was an odd feeling to rely on anyone, but she was getting accustomed to it. *Maybe too accustomed.*

She couldn't deny how she felt about him. Other than an occasional kiss, he hadn't made any big moves, but she could read the restless hunger in his eyes and had no problem interpreting it. After spending so much time with him, she'd begun to feel the same way. He gave the impression that he was only waiting for a sign that she would welcome a deepening of their relationship. Could she be ready to make that move? Men weren't that complicated—encouraging him could be as simple as stroking his arm.

She knew one thing—her body would vote hell, yes, despite not being completely healed. Feeling great in his company was the most important thing, though, and she certainly did.

Mulling her choices over, she went to move her mother's wooden box to a safe corner of the barn so she had enough room to work. She'd ordered a new hinge for it, but the custom piece still hadn't arrived . It required a special type of metal and the order was taking longer than expected. A few steps led to the intended destination, but on the last one, she tripped over her own feet and dropped the container. It hit the ground with a worrying thud, followed by the recognizable crack of wood splintering. "Oh, no," she muttered, followed by a few curses. Going to her knees, she checked the damage before picking it up. Although it remained mostly intact, one whole bottom corner had pulled away from the frame. A small nail protruded and some pages were sticking out of the opening. *What the heck?* Intrigued now, she pulled the whole box gingerly into her lap to inspect the damage.

When she worked the broken piece of wood free, she discovered a false bottom she hadn't known existed. Peering inside, she could see that the revealed space measured about six by nine inches and was about three inches deep. When she tugged what looked like papers free, she found they were contained in a soft, weathered, leather bound diary. With shaking hands, she opened it to find her mother's name scrawled across the front leaf. The pages were filled with faded, blue inked writing. Why hadn't she known her mother kept a diary? After the thought, she shook her head, feeling foolish. Why would any adult tell a child about their diary?

After dropping the box, she found she couldn't work on her projects after all. Curiosity about what secrets the diary held had her turning off the lights and closing up the barn for the night. She headed back to the cottage, her newfound treasure tucked under one arm. Once inside, she set it on the coffee table, showered and changed into cozy pajamas. She grabbed two cookies and a glass of milk, heading to the sofa. Switching on the outdated table lamp, she cuddled against one arm, opened the diary, and started reading.

Before too long, she realized her mother had started the diary when she got pregnant. When Harper jumped forward to the days after she was born, her mother spoke about the happiness her birth had brought, about learning to diaper and feed. Every day had a little milestone to savor. Some days, she wrote just a sentence or two, others, a page or more. Within ten pages, she referred to her hope that God would forgive her mistake. *What mistake?*

Although she continued to read, there was no immediate explanation. After a while, she yawned and put it down, vowing to continue reading tomorrow. Texting Aaron goodnight, she headed to bed.

## Chapter Eight

Aaron sat at his desk the next morning, mulling over the events of the previous day. He'd spent most of the time with his men yesterday, because he had two people out sick and had to cover their positions. That was the difference between working in a small department versus a large one. Circumstances sometimes required him to work, hands on, during a fire. He didn't mind it, though. It helped keep him in shape and on top of how well his men were working together.

Late in the evening, as he'd been finishing up some overdue paperwork, he received a phone call from one of his men. Apparently, Chief Johnson was kicked back in one of the local bars, disparaging Aaron and his department. He'd cautioned his man to ignore him. "He's not worth it," he said and was happy when his co-worker said he'd leave to avoid losing his temper. Sooner or later, the ridiculous drama over Rocky's firing would blow over. Unnecessary tantrums always did.

Talk of all that nonsense was more than he could deal with while tired and hungry, so he set it aside. He'd missed seeing Harper after work and was surprised that fact left him a little depressed. When he popped in this morning to see if she was doing well, she'd seemed a little withdrawn. He'd have to see if he could figure out what bothered her tonight.

A much quieter day meant that he caught up on all

of the waiting paperwork and left at six while his men sat down to eat their supper. Instead of heading straight for the shower as he normally did, he walked up the hill to see Harper. He found her just opening her front door. "Oh, you're home." She smiled up at him.

He felt relief at the sight of her, noting that she looked more relaxed. "I thought I'd see if you wanted some takeout. I'm too lazy to cook."

"Sure. How about pizza?"

"Sounds good. Why don't you come and chill out at my place? If you don't mind, I'll get you to order while I grab a shower."

"That's fine." Walking down the hill, she told him she'd finished both the bar cart and a bookcase. "I thought I might load them up and take them to the flea market tomorrow if you can help me lift them tonight or in the morning. My other things are already packed and ready to go."

"Am I invited to come with you?"

Surprise widened her eyes. "Of course. As long as you're sure you won't get bored. It can be slow at times."

"If I'm with you, I won't be." Her smile said his comment made her happy. *Good.*

She ordered him the extra-large triple meat special he'd asked for while she settled on an Alfredo with tomatoes. Her choice sounded boring as hell to him, but each to her own. When he emerged from his room after showering and dressing, he found her curled up against the pillows on the sofa. He decided to take the bull by the horns. "You were a little quiet this morning. Is everything okay?"

Meeting his gaze, she smiled, the warmth in her eyes reassuring him. "Yes. I'm sorry I worried you. I just discovered something yesterday that caught me by surprise." She told him about her clumsiness and how she'd found the diary.

"That's interesting. I always thought hidden compartments were something you only heard about in mystery novels."

"Me, too. So far, it's mostly stuff about being a mother, you know, everyday things. It's a little weird that she took such care to hide it, though. But now I wonder if she just she didn't want my father to see it."

"Why do I feel like you're leaving something out?"

She shrugged, trying to make light of it, but her body tensed. "She refers to a 'secret' which kind of freaked me out, but she never says what she's referring to. Not yet, anyway. I jumped ahead and read out of order, so tomorrow, I think I'll start from the very beginning and read a bit every day."

"I'm sure it's no big deal. Everyone has secrets and they usually only mean a lot to that person." He took a seat opposite her. "I'm sure you have a few yourself. Come on, spill. I won't tell anybody."

"I honestly can't think of even one. I guess I'm pretty boring."

"No secret crushes?" He wiggled his eyebrows, relieved when she met his gaze.

"I'm not sure it's much of a secret," she murmured, color creeping onto her cheeks.

His night just got much better at her words. "You could come sit on my lap and we could discuss our mutual crush." The front bell rang and he laughed. "Great timing as usual." He walked over and opened the door to find Tommy Farris on the step, balancing two pizza boxes.

Dianne McCartney

"Hey, Harper," the boy called, his eyes lighting.

"Hey, Tommy. How are your folks?"

"Good. They went bowling tonight."

"That means your dad's bad leg is feeling better. Glad to hear it."

Whipping his wallet from his back pocket, Aaron paid the boy and added a good tip. The teenager grinned his thanks, waved, and jogged back to his truck. Honking as he backed out, he sped off. He carried the boxes to the counter, and said, "Tommy's got a crush on you."

"Oh, please. He's barely eighteen and just out of high school."

"I've been a teenage boy and, believe me, you being older is not a problem for him. Not at all. More like a bonus." He dropped a kiss on her cheek as she joined him. "Grab some plates from that first cupboard, will you?"

They chowed down on the pizza until even he had to give up, groaning and rubbing his stomach. "I don't know why pizza tastes even better when someone else has to cook it."

"So true." She put the leftovers into the refrigerator, then curled up next to him on the couch. They watched about half of a movie before she put a hand on his thigh. He met her gaze, wondering if this was the sign he'd been waiting for, the one that signaled more serious interest. When she met his gaze, her eyes shining, he knew.

He didn't waste time with games. "Will you come to bed with me?"

"I would love to." She raised her casted arm. "I'm a bit of a lame dog at the moment, but I think we'll manage."

"I promise to take care of you." Grasping her hand, he led her to the bedroom. He undressed her slowly, each piece unveiling more of her curvy body. To him, she was like a work of art, all creamy skin with a light dusting of freckles. "You're beautiful," he whispered and her smile lit the room. When he got down to her sweet, white lingerie, she put a hand against his chest.

"You need to catch up." He helped her with his buttons and then watched, transfixed, as she undid his belt and zipper. Sucking in a breath, he tried not to moan as she slid his jeans carefully down until he could step out of them. She reached up to kiss him, her lips warm and welcoming. A minute later, their underthings joined the clothes on the floor. Stepping into his arms, she let her body meet his, and now, he did groan at how well she fit.

"I've been thinking about this for months," he whispered, taking her hand to lower her to the bed. When she scooted over, he joined her. Both pairs of hands traveled, seeking and learning what felt best to the other. When her good hand closed around him, he felt a rush of heat and returned the favor, relishing in the slick heat of her. He cradled her in his arms, making sure her bad arm stayed out of the way. In the end, making love to her was the most natural thing in the world. They met touch for touch, stroke to stroke, until they crashed and surrendered to ultimate pleasure.

"You feel so good," she said afterward, curling against his side. "Better than I could have dreamed."

"That's an understatement." He had no better words to describe such a connection, so he let it go. Kissing her, he tucked her under one arm and they fell asleep.

Aaron had worried that things might be awkward

between them in the morning, but, much to his relief, they weren't. It could be that having to get up and head for the flea market by six thirty was a good thing, even if it didn't feel like it when he dragged himself out from his warm spot next to her. He would much rather have stayed in bed with her, but he couldn't afford to be selfish. By the time they'd both showered and grabbed muffins, plus thermos cups with coffee, it was time to leave. The two pieces of furniture were loaded in three minutes and they were off, headed to the sprawling fairgrounds where the flea market took place. The cool morning air got them moving, but he knew it would warm up soon.

The big, wrought iron gates didn't open to customers until eight, so he was surprised to see the lineup of vendors had already started to form. A long line of trucks and trailers made a colorful column. "They don't assign vendor spots," Harper explained, "so it's a first come, first serve situation. If you're not here early, you'll be stuck way at the back where there's less foot traffic." She giggled. "One day, a group of teenagers took Mrs. Hanson's spot, the one that she's had for twenty years. She chased them away with her broom. It made quite a sight, because she's eighty-nine and stands maybe five feet tall at the most."

"Did she convince them to let her keep her spot?"

"Darn right. She swung that thing like a baseball legend would. The kids saw the wisdom of moving on."

Everyone seemed to be proceeding in an orderly fashion today, so that was reassuring. She drove up to one of the spots that was at a crossroads and parked her truck with the bed facing out. As she turned the ignition off, she explained. "This way, we can leave the furniture to be displayed on the bed of the truck. That means people can easily see the pieces, even from a distance." She slid out of the truck and he followed. "And, if we don't sell them, at least they're already loaded. Take it from me—carrying furniture and boxes when you're already tired from a busy day sucks."

"So, you just display the rest of the merchandise on the folding tables?"

"Exactly."

He wanted to be useful and not just sit around like a lump while she worked. "Okay. Why don't I put the tables in place and you can tell me where each box of items belongs? I'll leave the arrangements to you."

"That sounds perfect." They worked together in comfortable harmony. Her professional instincts impressed him. She even had a hand-carved wooden sign that read Harper's Home Goods that she displayed in the most visible corner. Business cards sat in a stack beside it. When she was finished setting up, he saw that she had made little vignettes featuring the different items. Her meticulous process intrigued and impressed him. She obviously knew what she was doing. Each area looked like what you'd see in a store window.

They sat and relaxed on a pair of folding chairs as they waited for the gates to open, a cash box and a credit card processor sitting on the little table she'd put in between them. He was surprised to hear that a lot of people still preferred to deal in cash and some dealers dealt in nothing else. "You can often get better bargains for cash," she said with a smile. "And, frankly, a lot of people don't claim the income. But, don't worry, mine is a business, so I keep excellent records. I'm far too paranoid to cheat the tax man."

He could tell when the front gates opened by the rushing horde that erupted down the main lane toward them, like cattle freed from metal chutes at a rodeo. A few of them were even jogging, scanning back and forth as they went. It was a wonder they didn't slam into one another. She laughed when he expressed surprise. "Everyone knows the best treasures disappear early." They even saw Dr. Mason jog by in athletic shoes and sneakers, darting around people as he went. A few minutes later, she said, "Batten down the hatches. Here they come." With a final reminder for him to keep an eye on the cash box, she stood up to greet the first customer. As time marched on, he watched with awe as she juggled multiple customers at a time, chatting away to all of them. Trying to help where he could, he wrapped the purchases for her, bagged them, and made change when necessary. Within two hours, over half her items were gone which surprised him. When he expressed admiration, she said, "I've been coming here a long time and always try to get the same booth, so I get a lot of repeat business. And I promote the most interesting items on social media. I've found that it makes a huge difference in sales."

Some of the customers were men wandering around on their own and he noticed they hung around a little longer than necessary. He bared his teeth at a few, half tempted to snarl, and they moved on. After their romantic interlude last night, he felt a little territorial. Or maybe a lot, which surprised him. It wasn't his usual style.

By one thirty, she had sold everything except three small items. The furniture pieces had sold within the first hour, both going to the same woman. They were going to deliver them for the happy buyer on the way home. Declaring it an excellent sales day, she told him it was time to have some fun. Covering the delivery items with blankets and then a tarp, she secured them with ropes. The small items got locked in the truck. Free to relax and enjoy themselves, they wandered off to find some food for a late lunch.

She talked him into monster glasses of lemonade freezes and hefty chicken sandwiches made with thick slices of fresh baked bread which were surprisingly tasty. Afterward, he talked her into enjoying some homemade ice cream. They ate it, moaning in pleasure as they tried to capture all the drips before they fell. Once they'd finished, they strolled up and down the aisles. As they walked, he took her hand, pleased when she allowed him. She'd been a little skittish about being seen as a couple in public at first. "I didn't realize how many different items there would be for sale here."

"I know what you mean. You could furnish your whole house, supply it with the extras and outfit your kids if you wanted to. All of that at a much lower price than you'd pay in normal stores." He helped her case out the other vendors and dig through various piles for buried treasure. She unearthed a few interesting salvage items, made of both wood and metal, and he carried them back to the truck for her. By late afternoon, they were dropping off the sold furniture at the purchaser's place and heading home.

That evening, they relaxed on the deck, sipping beer as the sun sank lower in the sky. He gave Harper a blanket to pull over her legs. "You never told me how you came to be a firefighter. Was it what you wanted when you were a kid?"

He knew she'd ask at some point, so he was prepared. It was a painful story, but he wanted to share his personal history with her. "No, I thought I wanted to be a policeman, actually."

"Why did you change your mind?"

"I guess you could say reality changed it for me. I did well in the academy and was a cop for four years. One night, my partner got killed during a robbery and everything changed for me."

She stretched her hand out to grasp his, squeezing it. "I'm so sorry. I had no idea or I wouldn't have asked."

It amazed him that nothing felt awkward with her. "It's okay. I want us to know more about each other's lives. The memories still get to me, so I don't talk about it much."

"You don't have to. You can tell me some other time."

"No, I've been wanting to tell you." He took a deep breath to steady himself. "He was ten years older than me, had one kid already and another on the way. The robber was only seventeen. Right when Rich thought he was lowering the gun, the kid panicked, shooting everything in sight. A random shot caught my partner, just above his vest. He died on scene after asking me to look out for his family."

She climbed out of her chair without a word and came over to settle on his lap. Instead of offering meaningless condolences, she just held him, rubbing her lips against his cheek. The comfort her simple gesture offered astounded him. An unprecedented sense of peace settled around them. His feelings for her grew every day and her touch both stimulated and comforted him. He only hoped she would feel the same way. After a few moments, she whispered, "Did you quit right after that?"

"Pretty much. I was barely muddling through, trying to get past the nightmares when I met a fire chief one night. We hit it off right away. After we hung out a few times, I think he realized I was struggling with what I should do. He suggested that the fire department might be a better fit for me." He blew out a breath. "Thank goodness, he was right. I rode along with him on some calls to observe for a few days. then quit the police department and signed up. After training, I worked really hard under my mentor for eight years. After that, he made me his assistant. This job came open two years later. I was still pretty young to become a chief, but the choice of applicants was slim and I got lucky. A lot of firefighters want to work in the city. Some might find small towns boring, but it's the perfect situation for me." He smiled. "And it keeps me close to my family."

"How is your friend's family doing?"

"Kathy remarried and moved away. I still get birthday and Christmas cards from her and the kids which I enjoy."

"You're a kind and thoughtful man."

He decided it was time to raise the mood to a happier place. "And, is kindness sexy?"

Nodding, she said, "It is to me. That and a sense of humor are the two most important qualities in a person as far as I'm concerned."

"Oh, good. You had me worried for a minute." He lifted her chin and kissed her. Her enthusiastic response had him lifting her and carrying her to bed.

Chapter Nine

In the morning, Aaron talked to Harper as she exited the shower, a towel wrapped around her. He knew he should have mentioned this plan the night before, but he hadn't wanted to scare her off. "I hope you're ready to meet my mom. She and my sister, Sammy, are coming by in a while."

Whirling, she stared at him, shock making her gape. "What time?"

"Not this very minute." He glanced at the watch he'd just strapped on his wrist. "In about an hour."

"Oh, my gosh." Her eyes bugged out. "Why on earth didn't you tell me?" Ripping the protective plastic off her cast, she threw it out, droplets of water hitting the carpet.

"I just did." She started to scrabble for her clothes and her frantic demeanor made him laugh out loud. "Calm down. It's not like they're charging through the bedroom door this instant. There's no big rush."

She paused to grimace. "I want to look presentable when I meet them and that takes time." Shoving her legs into her jeans, she chucked the towel aside, letting it fall to the carpet. "Where the heck did you throw my blouse last night?"

He pointed to the opposite corner where it lay crumpled on the floor. "Relax. They're every bit as casual as we are. They're going to love you."

Huffing out an exasperated breath, she said, "They

usually don't love me, you know. Other women never think I'm girly enough. And you've hardly ever told me anything about them. What are we supposed to talk about?" Having picked up her rumpled top, she threaded her cast in first, then pushed her arms through her sleeves. Spying her underpants lying on the floor, she stuffed them in her pocket.

"You can talk about me." He flexed one arm and posed, feeling rewarded when she rolled her eyes. As she buttoned her blouse, he teased, "They might be a little nosy about our relationship, but I'm sure you can handle it. You've already dealt with the town gossips. My family will be easy in comparison."

"Why will they be nosy? Are they worried you're just a boy toy?" She plopped down on the bed to pull on her sneakers.

"You can play with me any time," he offered.

She responded with a snort of derision. "Oh, don't be such a man. I'm being serious here."

He shouldn't get a kick about how flustered she was getting, but it proved hard not to poke fun at her concerns. "You're worrying about nothing. After they leave, you'll wonder why you made such a big deal about a simple visit. Sammy will just tell you what a pain in the butt I am and you can agree." He watched as she scanned the room. "What are you looking for?"

"I want to make sure they won't find any damning evidence of me in here."

"Are you worried about ruining my reputation?" He took a few steps and ran his hands down her arms in an attempt to soothe her. "They're not going to search my bedroom." At least he hoped not. "And what if they did? We're both adults and long past the age of consent."

"I guess. I'm just not used to having family around. Especially one I want to impress." After a pause, she said, "I need to get into fresh clothes, though. Should I come back or just stay at my place until you're ready for me?"

He kissed her forehead. "Come back, of course, whenever you're done." After she left, he watched through the window. He shook his head, laughing when she jogged up the hill as if terriers nipped at her heels. He was tempted to take a photo of her panties poking out of her pocket, but figured that might take teasing too far. Thirty minutes later, he was glad she'd made her escape, because his family showed up a little early as was their habit. Harper would have freaked out if they caught her getting dressed at his place. He figured she'd better get used to it. He wanted her next to him whenever he could manage it.

Climbing out of the car, his mother and sister could have passed for twins at a distance. Both were leggy blondes, their long hair piled in an easy knot on their heads. Their usual uniform of jeans and buttoned-down shirts was expected. His sister strode over first, grinning as she peeked behind him. "Well, where's your new roommate?"

"Oh, for heaven's sake, Sammy, give your brother a minute to breathe." His mom reached up to kiss his cheek, straightening his collar. "How are you, sweetie?"

"I'm great. And, in answer to your question, Harper's in the cottage, getting changed. Come inside. She'll be down in a minute." They'd arrived armed with an assortment of frozen food in plastic containers which he stacked in the freezer, thanking them. He often wondered if they thought he would starve to death without their contributions, but he knew they did it out of love and felt grateful for their thoughtfulness. They settled in the living room and, after only a few minutes, he heard Harper rap on his door. "Come in," he hollered and rose to greet her. The sober look on her face told him she was still intimidated by the prospect of meeting them. He took her hand and felt it tremble as the others stood to greet her. "Mom, Sammy, this is Harper."

She nodded a hello. "Sammy, Mrs. Lassiter. It's nice to meet you both." Her hands clutched together until his mother pulled her in for a warm hug.

"Oh, honey, call me Meredith. Everyone does."

She smiled as she pulled back, her shoulders relaxing. "Thank you, I will." Following Aaron to the sofa, they all re-took their seats and she sank down beside him. "Sammy, Aaron never told me what you do for a living."

"I teach grade four at the local elementary school."

"Oh, you must have the patience of a saint. I loved my teachers when I was a kid, but I know I asked way too many questions."

"Actually, the parents sometimes require more patience than the kids. Parent's night is my least favorite night of the year." And that's all it took for the conversation to flow. They discussed school, Meredith's hat making and eventually the discussion turned to Harper's work. When his family was told what she did, they demanded to see her projects.

"Well, for starters, look at my new coffee table." He gestured toward it with pride.

His mother's jaw dropped. "You made this? It's stunning. I hope you made him pay dearly for it."

Harper narrowed her gaze. "I wanted him to take it

as a gift to thank him for all the wonderful support he's given me, but he wouldn't hear of it."

"Good. Then I raised him right."

"Oh, there's no doubt about that. He's always so thoughtful."

"That's always wonderful for a mother to hear. It helps us forgive them when they screw up." She seemed to enjoy his yelp of protest. "Can we see more of your work?" His mother, especially, seemed eager so they all filed out to the barn where she had a few projects in progress. Meredith looked around with glee. Harper explained the other pieces had sold at the flea market and told them about her online site. "You're very talented, honey. I'd love to have this kind of creative vision."

As expected, she blushed, but he could tell she appreciated the compliment. After they closed up the barn, they decided to drive to Momma Sue's for an early lunch. The casual spot boasted the best fried chicken and milkshakes found around here and was apparently the ladies' favorite. Once there, they grabbed a circular booth at the back and slid onto the vinyl bench seats. After they ordered, Sammy said, "So, how long have you and my brother been dating?"

Harper grabbed her water glass and took a big gulp. He answered for her. "For about a month. Harper only decided I was worth the risk after her house caught fire."

She looked horrified at his joke. "Don't listen to him. He's teasing. I was just…giving it some thought."

Meredith laughed. "That means you have discerning taste. A young lady should always consider the inherent risks of giving a man a chance. We have to be sure we're getting the prince version of a man, not the toad."

"Oh, thanks, Mom." Aaron did his best to look

disgruntled which made them laugh.

"You're welcome. What happened with the fire, anyway? Have you found the arsonist yet?"

He shook his head. "Still working on it, but no luck so far. Arson is a challenging crime to solve. There are so many variables." He'd finish his thought, but he didn't want to say much more. "Most arsonists are young males, but there are exceptions. And a lot are employed in menial jobs, but not all of them. Ty's helping, but we're not getting very far." Within a few minutes, lunch was served and they moved on to more benign subjects.

After they went home with full bellies, his family prepared to leave. "Oh, I forgot one thing." Meredith dashed to the car and returned with a medium-sized brown box. "I brought you a little something." She handed the package to Harper.

"For me?" she gasped, her eyes wide. Aaron hadn't considered that having no family meant no presents. He would have to remedy that.

"Of course. It's just a little treat. Open it." His mother waited for Harper's reaction, looking expectant.

She set it on the kitchen counter and raised the lid. A deep blue hat lay nestled among the crisp, white tissue. "Oh, my gosh." She lifted it carefully out and Meredith helped her put it on. They all followed her to the bathroom mirror so she could see her reflection. The color brought out the tone of her eyes, deepening the gentle blue. "It's b-beautiful. No one has ever given me such a lovely gift. Thank you so much."

"You're so welcome. Aaron gave me an estimate on the size of your head and showed me a picture of you, so I'm glad he was right." They all traded hugs and the other women left, leaving the two of them alone together.

"I told you they'd like you." He gave her a minute to rub the tears from her eyes.

She turned to hug him, releasing a breath. "You're really lucky, you know. They're both wonderful."

"Believe me, I'm aware. Even Sammy liked you and she's pretty outspoken and opinionated. You'd know it right off if she didn't approve." They spent the afternoon doing a few errands and then watched a movie before heading to bed.

**** 

By chance, the arsonist had overheard that the fire chief and his new hire had been nosing around his last fire in Springvale. Now, brewing anger made him restless. Lighting fires in different locales had saved him from being caught up to this point, but he didn't want anyone, especially Aaron, taking a closer look. Mind you, the fact that he didn't fit the profile of a typical arsonist didn't hurt. They would focus on young boys and other losers while he lounged in his expensive home and drank top notch brandy, laughing at them.

Still, it didn't pay to get lax. Since the fire, he'd discovered that the young fire chief had worked for a city department before coming here. That meant his knowledge was likely superior to the average fireman you usually found in a Podunk town like this. And both his curiosity and his instincts might pose a real threat to his freedom. That couldn't be allowed.

Part of the reason he'd remained in this town after all these years was that the likelihood of being caught was low to non-existent. If that changed, he might have to re-evaluate all possible options. For now, what he desperately needed was a distraction. Maybe another fire, closer to home. Could he lure Harper anyway nearby or was it too soon? He didn't know.

But it was certainly an idea worth considering.

## Chapter Ten

When all the assorted chores at the firehouse were finished, and there were no current fires to deal with, Rocky helped Aaron look for similar suspicious fires in the surrounding counties. There were a few that looked linked to their arson and a couple of other possibilities, but the fire scenes wouldn't yield clues at this late date. All they had at this point was a working theory. If the fires were, in fact, connected, clearly the arsonist had spread his sites around in an attempt to evade detection. Until now, the sneaky plan had worked.

At the same time, he had heard whispers that Arne was over-extended financially. The owner of Harper's rental was, according to what he'd heard, quite fond of gambling and had suffered an extended losing streak. Was there any possibility that he had set the fire himself? It would hardly be the first time someone used an insurance check to net some ready cash, but that theory seemed off to him. As unlikeable as the man was, Aaron still didn't see his problems as a reason for burning a house that was bringing in regular revenue. Just the same, he would have Ty check his alibi of being on a work trip out of town.

Which one of their theories rang true? Or were they off track with both of them?

****

Harper felt like a total klutz. While working on a set

of drawers, she had jammed her finger and then tore her skin open on an old, previously undetected nail. Blood dripped all over her shirt as she hurried across to the cottage to wash the wound out and put hydrogen peroxide on it for good measure. She clenched her teeth as those evil, cleaning bubbles hit the open wound. Her tetanus shot was up to date, thank goodness, so she wouldn't have to worry about that possibility. A vaccination was essential when she handled old metal pieces all the time. She tried to be careful, but accidents happened.

Wrapping cotton pads around the digit, tight, she bandaged it. The bleeding finally slowed to a mere drip which left dark shadows against the dressing. Grabbing a cold drink from the refrigerator afterward, she carried it back up to the barn. Before she made it to the door, a motion caught her peripheral vision. She turned to see a small, black car crawling past on the road. When she stared at it, it picked up speed and disappeared in a cloud of dust. Unable to see who sat behind the wheel, she shrugged. *Probably someone searching for an address.*

Forgetting all about it, she got back to work. At supper time, she heard the sound of a truck and poked her head out to see Aaron coming to a halt by the house. He climbed up the hill to join her. Taking his hat off, he wiped his brow. "How was your day?"

Holding up her bandaged hand, she said, "Other than slicing my one useful hand like an idiot, I'm good." She told him what had happened.

"You cleaned it though, right? Are you sure you don't need stitches?"

His concern warmed her heart. She shook her head. "It's not deep. Fingers just bleed a lot. And, yes, I have my tetanus shot, so don't worry." Gesturing inside, she said, "I think I'm done for the day. Do you want me to cook us some dinner?"

"Not likely, since you no longer have one healthy hand, but there's no need. Mrs. Langston came by to thank us for putting out the grass fire near their place last week. She brought three different casseroles for the men and included one for me to take home." He grinned. "She said she brought it for me and the young lady I'm sweet on. Apparently, our relationship was the main topic for discussion at the hair salon yesterday."

"That better be me she's referring to, because I'm eating it, regardless. I'm hungry."

"Oh, that's definitely you." He waited as she put away her tools and then he closed the barn doors, locking them.

"I need to take a shower before dinner." She plucked her sweaty shirt away from her body, grimacing.

He pulled her close. "What a coincidence. So do I. Want to conserve some water?"

"Absolutely." They continued down the hill together. Needless to say, dinner was late and she never thought to mention the passing car.

****

The arsonist wasn't too pleased that Harper had caught him casing Aaron's property. It figures. Any other time she would have been busy inside the house or the barn. Getting caught was just a bit of bad luck. After mulling it over, though, he relaxed. Although she'd noticed his car, he didn't think she'd recognized him from that big a distance. She hadn't seemed particularly concerned about it, either. That fact irked him more than anything. He wanted her to at least be a little paranoid, shaky enough to keep constantly looking over her shoulder. She'd barely escaped the inferno and now she was playing house with Aaron, looking comfortable and at home. *Damn it!* She didn't deserve to be happy.

He would have to discover if she used any tools that could potentially create a fire hazard. That way, she wouldn't look like a victim, she'd look careless. If he could find a way for her to be blamed for both Arne's fire and a fire at Aaron's, surely people would begin to doubt her. There were always people around to spread ridiculous theories. The compelling idea required further thought.

Harper came from a long line of intriguing women. Her mother had been the love of his life. Having fallen for her at first sight, he would have given anything to have met her before he made the mistake of marrying Susan. Still, the two of them had cherished the time they'd had together, managing to avoid both his wife and her husband to meet in clandestine fashion wherever possible. Stolen moments had yielded a combustible affair wrought in unparalleled passion until her unplanned pregnancy. Harper's arrival had ruined everything. He didn't want children and the love of his life knew it. Her pregnancy and the eventual birth brought a screeching halt to the only happiness he'd ever known.

And, after that, his life had crumbled to ruins. A fickle fate had delivered series of unrelenting blows that changed his life forever. He lost his wife, his lover and his home in one disastrous week. Susan threw him out, cashed out in every way possible, and moved away. She'd never spoken to him again. He'd never believed in the concept of an evil seed until that horrific day.

It was Harper's fault. And that single fact made it long past time that she paid a daunting penalty for the crime of her birth.

\*\*\*\*

Harper sat alone in the cottage's living room, paging through the worn leaves of her mother's journal. The leather was so old that it creaked as she split the pages to catch up to the section where she'd last stopped. Faded ink meant she only read a short section each evening because her mother's cursive was difficult to read at times. Her outlook had turned dark at the last entry and Harper hadn't yet figured out the reason for her rapid change of mood. She'd mentioned depression creeping into her daily life. Harper finally found the place she'd stopped reading the previous night.

*Diary*

*I spent the afternoon on my knees, praying for absolution from a reluctant God. If Dale ever finds out about my secret, I'm doomed. He would never forgive me. And I find it almost impossible to forgive myself.*

*I am trying to be an excellent mother to Harper. She is such a lovely child, full of smiles and sweetness. Do I deserve her? Probably not. But I will work harder to be worthy of her in the future. I know my sins can't be wiped away simply because I am contrite. All I can do is try to become a better person, one more worthy of her love.*

*In the meantime, J has become unpredictable and he's beginning to frighten me. He lost his wife and his house, despite the fact that we parted ways. I'm not sure how Susan found out about us. It doesn't really matter now, anyway. But I saw him watching me from the road the other day, just standing there, staring, as if one glance could turn me into stone. It unnerved me. I sent a note to his work address, warning him to stay away, but he won't listen. The gossips whisper in town, wondering about why he's struggling. I hear their murmurs. I'm the only one who knows the reason behind his destructive behavior.*

*All I can do is pray that he moves on with his life. Soon, before he ruins mine.*

The entry ended there.

Shocked, Harper closed the diary with shaky fingers. Her mother had an affair. It went against everything she'd known about her. She'd always thought her mom and dad had been happy together before her birth. Maybe that was what children of troubled families always thought. But this confession might explain why her father had taken off, never to be seen again. Could that be why her father couldn't bear to look at her after that?

She gasped in a breath. Could the other man be her real father? The thought made her stomach hurt. Adoring the man she knew as her father had made the pain so much worse when he left. What if it was all an earth-shattering lie?

For a moment, she wished that her mother's box had burned in the fire. If it had, she wouldn't have all these unanswered questions now. And there was nobody to answer them, no one she could rely on to tell her the truth. She had no idea where her father had gone. He'd made no attempt to contact her in all these years. Was he even still alive? No way to know.

Her call buzzed with an incoming text, tearing her from her thoughts. It was Aaron.

*—Want me to get takeout?—*

After a few moments' thought, she answered.

*—I'm a little tired tonight. I think I'm just going to go to bed early. Thanks anyway.—*

*—Are you feeling okay?—*

*—Fine. Just tired—*

She knew he'd wonder what was going on with her, but she felt too upset to discuss what she'd found. *Maybe in the morning.* Drinking a glass of milk to hold her through the night, she climbed into bed. Wrapping the quilt around her, she shut her eyes and hoped sleep would finally come.

\*\*\*\*

Aaron drove home, his lonely dinner for one packaged in a to-go box on the seat beside him. Trying not to feel rejected, he was failing miserably. He shouldn't take it to heart. The two of them had been together every night for a while. It wasn't like her to not tell him how she was feeling. She seemed a little subdued, as if something troubled her.

He'd give her some space, though. Apparently, she needed a bit of time on her own. He couldn't help, but wonder what had changed her mood. Once he arrived home, the quiet of the house bothered him. He usually loved it after a busy day, but everything had changed with Harper's arrival. Coming home to some company, her company at least, made him happier than he could have ever imagined. He wondered, for the first time, if his days as a bachelor were numbered. If she knew the direction of his thoughts, would it please her or frighten her away?

After chewing down his dinner, which now tasted like old leather, he gave himself a kick in the butt. They were separate for just one night, for heaven's sake. In the morning, he would knock on her door to check and make sure she was okay. When he turned the television on, his usual shows bored him silly. He finally clicked it off, grabbed a book, and headed to bed to read, hoping the words would lull him to sleep.

Morning found him blinking in confusion, wondering for a minute where Harper was and why she wasn't wrapped around him. Then he remembered her desire for alone time. Swiping the paperback off his chest, he rose and got ready for the day. He showered and dressed as if on automatic. As he stood at the counter, eating some toast and mulling over the situation, he saw her kitchen light switch on. *Good.* He hadn't wanted to wake her, but felt as if they should talk, just so he wouldn't worry.

He pulled on his jacket and hat, grabbed his keys and locked up. Heading up the hill, he saw her figure cross in front of the window. She opened the door, dredging up a smile. "Good morning."

"Are you feeling okay?"

"Yes. Sorry about last night. I just felt a little out of sorts."

He met her gaze. "No need to be sorry. I just wanted to make sure that you were all right."

"I'm fine. I just…" She shifted to lean against the doorframe. "I found something upsetting in my mother's dairy and I'm trying to digest it, I guess."

"It might help to talk to me about it. I'm a good listener."

"Can we do that after work? If I talk about it now, I'm going to get all teary again and I just got rid of a headache."

"Of course, we can." He squeezed her hand. "Whatever you need, I'll be here for you. You know that, right?"

"I do know that." Stepping forward, she put her arms around his waist and hugged him tighter than normal. "Be careful at work."

Leaning down, he kissed her, softly, on the lips. "You call me if you need anything. Anything at all."

"I will, but don't worry, I'll be fine." Aaron took a lingering look as he walked to his truck. Climbing in, he started the ignition, belting up. He watched her in the rearview window until he turned the corner onto the road.

They were blessed with a quiet morning at work. The well-rested men thought they were in for another quiet day until a call came in at quarter to three. One engine headed out while he followed in the SUV. It was an address he recognized, owned by some young deadbeat parents Ty was familiar with because of their frequent domestic disturbance calls. Hopefully, the family were all out of the house and not inside.

When they rolled on scene, the first floor of the house was fully engulfed, flames visible through the front windows. As he shouted commands to the men, he paused to ask the circle of watching neighbors if they knew if anyone was home. "He and the wife took off about thirty minutes ago," an older man said, stepping forward. "I saw them leave. Not sure about the boy, though. I've called the sheriff's department more than once about him being left alone to fend for himself."

"How old is he?"

"Seven or eight." Aaron sent up a quick prayer that he hadn't made it home from school yet. He yelled to his men about the possibility of a child being present and kept an eye on them as they worked to beat the flames back. The first floor was fully involved, but it hadn't reached the second level yet. He'd no sooner thanked God for that than a boy's panicked face appeared at one of the upstairs windows. The watching women started to scream and point in his direction. Rocky saw him at the same time and handed off his hose to another man. He heard Aaron's shouted order and snatched a ladder from the truck. Supporting it against the still solid roof of the front porch, he began to climb. The other men had their hands full fighting the blaze, so Aaron ran to join him, steadying it as the younger man vaulted up the steps, then stepped onto the still secure porch roof.

Because of the steep angle, Aaron could see and hear everything Rocky said and did. "Stand back! I'm going to break the window. Cover your face." His words were barely heard, over the noise, but the boy obeyed. Rocky smashed the window and, after being coaxed, the boy launched himself through the newly created hole toward him. "Watch the glass!" He lifted him clear of the jagged edges, stepping surely to the edge where the ladder waited. His foot slipped and he went down on one knee, but kept the boy firmly anchored against his chest. Aaron reached up to take the boy down the last few steps, allowing his firefighter to descend. The boy, dressed in holey jeans and a dirty shirt, coughed. He handed him off to the waiting ambulance attendants and went to check Rocky who was bent double, catching his breath.

"You okay?"

Pulling off his mask, he said, "Yes, Chief."

"Get the EMTs to check out that knee."

"I'm fine."

"That's an order. We don't take any risks with safety."

He shook his head in disgust. "The boy should have still been at school."

"I agree, but, obviously, the parents don't give a damn. I doubt education is their priority." He pointed at the ambulance. "Now, get going."

By the time the fire was finally out, Aaron figured that, even though most of the second floor was still standing, the insurance people would write the house off. Too much of the basic support system had been damaged. It wouldn't be safe to investigate until tomorrow, but he had an uneasy feeling about this fire, too. The damage was far more severe than it should have been. And, this time, it involved a child. Was the arsonist upping his stakes, not caring that a child might have died? That was a serious concern. An arsonist aimed at Harper was bad enough. An arsonist randomly targeting others terrified him. It would make his activities much harder to track.

The next day, after the ashes had cooled, he and Rocky examined the burned-out shell of the house. As expected, they discovered a similar pattern of burn marks to what they found at Harper's. He recorded the charred interior in minute detail and Rocky took photographs to back it up. "Why in hell would this guy light up a house when there's a kid home?"

"Maybe he didn't realize anyone was around."

"That's possible. Maybe he was watching as they drove away and assumed the kid was with the parents," the younger man mused. "If Harper was the intended target, how are she and this kid connected? Or are they?"

"Damned if I know. I'll ask her tonight. At this point, your guess is as good as mine." The lack of progress on this case frustrated Aaron. The answer to who was behind this had to be somewhere in Harper's history. The memory of her mother's diary came to mind. Any chance they might find a clue there? He didn't see how, but, at this point, anything was worth a shot.

****

Panic had the arsonist leaning against a wall in the foyer of his home, panting like a winded dog. He had stayed longer than he should have after he realized his horrendous mistake. There'd been an innocent child in the house. Slumping to the polished wood floor, he felt a stab of regret that cut right through his chest. He hadn't meant for anyone else to get entangled in his plans. He wasn't a monster. When the idiot parents left, he never dreamed that the child would be abandoned there, alone. At eight, he was much too young for that. Did they have no common sense?

Thank God, the firemen had saved him.

No one had ever been trapped in his fires before this, unless he'd meant them to be there. Well, no innocent person, anyway. He was meticulous, making sure that never happened. Harper had been, and still was, his only current goal. Thrilled by the leaping fire, he'd almost lost his lunch when he spied the child's face, heard those idiot women screaming like demented banshees. He should have left earlier, but like the other onlookers, he'd watched with bated breath as they retrieved him. After they had, he made his escape, blending in with the rest of the crowd to avoid notice before he slipped away. He'd trembled as he drove home, the shock of it ruining his night.

It was his job to save people, not to put them at risk. Guilt joined acid to burn a whole in his stomach. He searched for something to take that draining feeling away as he breathed in the appalling stench of his clothes.

It was Harper's fault. Trying to get rid of her had taken its toll on his mental health, that's all. It wasn't him. Instead, it represented just another sign that her toxic presence was doomed to ruin everything. He couldn't really be blamed for any of it.

Chapter Eleven

Harper wandered through one of the tempting aisles at the grocery store, trying to decide what to bake next for Aaron and his men. They plowed through her treats like industrial vacuums. Hearing that they were begging for more had become a weekly occurrence. It might seem silly to anyone else, but their pleas made her happy. Aaron wouldn't accept anything for rent except utility costs which were minimal. She'd even received her renter's insurance check to ease her financial situation, but he was holding firm. So, being able to supply him and the guys with plenty of baked goods was a way of giving back in return for everything he'd done to help her.

Chocolate chip cookies were always a favorite as were her peanut butter fudge bars. Maybe a cake would be a nice change. Moving her cart to one side, she investigated the boxes to choose a flavor. Startled when someone tapped her on the shoulder, she reacted by jerking away. Looking up, she was shocked to see an old boyfriend. "John! What on earth are you doing here?"

He laughed, running a hand through his cropped, blond hair. At sixty, he still looked good, but she couldn't say she missed her one and only age-gap lover. Hair dye and delusion probably still worked for him as it always had. "I didn't mean to startle you." The well-cut sports jacket, shirt and khakis he wore matched his taste from earlier years. He called his look professor camouflage. "I couldn't believe it was really you. Is this where you live now?"

"Yes. Are you just passing through?"

"No. I accepted an offer from the community college in Springvale. A co-worker told me this grocery has a better selection of food, and it's only twenty minutes away, so I thought I'd give it a try. Where are you working?"

"Actually, I have my own furniture and accessory recycling business here in town."

"Well, that must be…fun. I'd expected you to have given that up by now." He'd never been too impressed by what he called her *little hobby* and apparently that hadn't changed. "Why don't we have dinner tonight and catch up?"

In John's vernacular, dinner was code for feeding another kind of hunger and she was glad to have an excuse to bow out. She had a firm rule; no dating reruns, ever, especially when it came to arrogant men like him. "I'm sorry, John. I'm seeing someone and he's expecting me home for dinner."

"Home? You're living together?" The amusement in his gaze annoyed her.

Harper felt like saying "none of your business," but managed to hold back out of civility. "More or less." She hoped Aaron wouldn't mind making their situation seem serious enough to warn John off. Interest in anyone else had waned as soon as she'd spent time with Aaron.

"What does this paragon of virtue do?" The look in his eyes and his condescending words told her he didn't believe her.

"Aaron's the fire chief here in town."

He smirked. "That's a little blue collar for you, isn't it? You used to have more sophisticated tastes."

And, now, she remembered another reason she'd stopped dating him. That and the fact that his body parts tended to wander toward other women with little or no provocation. She wanted to snap at him, but settled for, "He's a wonderful man. I'm very lucky to have him in my life." He continued to yammer in her ear, but she tuned him out, having finally had enough. Grabbing what she needed for both cookies and cake, she headed to the front. Persistent to the end, he followed her through the checkout, continuing to haunt her to the sliding doors until she walked away, waving. She felt his eyes trained on her as she loaded her things, climbed into her truck and drove away.

****

Tuckered out from work, Aaron stopped for a few groceries on his way home. Rita Kent checked him out, the cashier's plain face beaming a toothy smile. According to Ty, she'd worked here as long as anyone could remember. "Well, there you are, Chief. Looking for your girlfriend?"

"Nope. Headed home, actually. Why?"

"Oh, she was here about an hour ago, picking up a few baking items. A good-lookin' man trailed her out, talking up a storm. Some older guy from the city, I guess. I sure didn't recognize him." She poked his arm, raising one eyebrow. "Better watch out, now. I know you don't want any competition. He looked all slicked up and ready to flirt."

He wondered who she was referring to, but didn't want to encourage her to further speculation. "I'm not too worried, but thanks for your concern. She'll be waiting, so I'd better hustle." Picking up his bags, he headed out. Not really being the jealous sort, he still wondered who Rita would have seen that she didn't recognize. That woman knew the business of everyone in town. It seemed to be her only claim to fame.

He arrived home ten minutes later, more than ready to relax. Harper wandered down from the cottage when she saw him unloading groceries. "Can I help?"

He grabbed the sacks, sliding two onto each arm. "No, I got them. Follow me in, though, and tell me how your day went." She trailed him inside and watched as he put his items away, teasing him about his meticulous organizational system. He waited for a pause, then felt compelled to ask, "Rita Kent tells me you ran into a friend at the grocery today?"

"Honestly, that woman must have supersonic ears. Either that or she has the whole store bugged." She laughed. "Yes, I ran into this guy I used to know in university."

"A fellow student? What's his name?"

"John Sutton. Actually, he's not a student. He taught a few of my classes first year."

"So, he's older than you?"

"Yes. Probably close to sixty by now."

"Someone you dated? She said he was flirting a little."

She wrinkled her nose. "We dated a few times, but it didn't work out. Why?"

"Rita mentioned his interest, that's all. I guess I'm just looking too hard at everyone after the fire. Did you break it off or did he?"

"I did. But he didn't seem to be at all broken-hearted. He slept with someone behind my back. After we broke up, I think he took another new girl out the very next night." She put her arms around his waist. "You're not jealous, are you?"

"I'm jealous of any man who knew you before me. And the age difference surprises me a little."

She grimaced. "Everyone makes a mistake now and then. He was mine. Believe me, I learned my lesson."

He dropped a gentle kiss on her forehead. "He didn't ask you out again, did he?"

"Well…he asked, but I said no. I told him I was seeing someone."

"And how did he react to that piece of information?"

"He blabbed on for a while, then said he'd see me later." She squeezed him. "And stop worrying. He's the last guy I would ever suspect of starting a fire with me in it. I suspect I was just one in a long stream of much younger women for him."

"Is he living here now?"

"Springvale, I guess. At least, that's where he's working, so I assume so. He got a job at the community college." She raised her eyebrows. "Seems like an odd fit for him, but, each to his own."

"What do you mean, an odd fit?" One town over wasn't far away enough as far as he was concerned. He was pleased that she didn't seem at all interested in this guy, but he felt compelled to learn a few basics about him.

"Well, he was quite well known in his field. No offense, but Springvale would be a pretty low-key choice for him."

His curiosity won out. "Why did you break up with him? I know I shouldn't dig into your business, but I'm curious."

"He's a little intense for me, I guess." She shrugged. "I always felt like I was under a microscope when I was around him. And he wasn't faithful, either. That's a total deal breaker for me."

"Yeah, me too." Aaron made a note of his name, planning to ask Ty to look into him. The timing of his appearance seemed suspect. And having her describe him as intense set off alarm bells. Harper didn't elaborate. He didn't want to alarm her, though, so he changed the subject. After dinner, they settled back on the couch. "Do you want to tell me why you were upset last night?"

She nibbled at her lip, her habit when she was tense. "I found out that my mother had an affair during her marriage to my father."

"Oh, that's upsetting." Now, he understood her unsettled mood last night. "Do you know when it happened?"

"A while before I was born. If I read between the lines, it sounds as if the pregnancy is what made her re-assess her life."

He decided to tread carefully, not wanting to upset her further. This could bring up a lot of troubling questions, but she might never find any reassuring answers. "Did she say who the other person was?"

"No. She just referred to him as the letter J. Why didn't she just say his name?"

"Probably to protect him in case the diary was ever found." He sighed. "I'm sorry, honey. Try not to think less of her. We can't know what was going on in your parents' lives at the time."

"She was a really good mom. I guess it shocked me. She felt a lot of guilt about it and talks about hoping for forgiveness." She looked up at him, her eyes somber. "At least I know why my dad took off, anyway. He must have been so upset."

"So, you think he knew?"

"Probably. It makes sense, doesn't it? He found out and it broke his heart."

"It's still not an excuse for leaving you behind." Abandoning your child is something Aaron would never understand. Ending a troubled marriage was one thing, but it was a parent's duty to protect any children they brought into the world.

"I know. It sounds like Mom decided to stay with Dad because of me. But, part of me wonders if I might be her lover's child and she just couldn't face the scandal of that."

"Don't jump to conclusions. If you were, why wouldn't she have just left your father to be with him? That would make more sense."

"I don't know." She gave a big sigh. "It's all so confusing. Maybe when I get further into the diary, I'll learn more."

Leaning over, he grabbed her hand and squeezed. "Maybe you'd be happier just leaving it be. I hate to see you this upset."

"As strange as it probably sounds, I think I'd rather know the truth. I can forgive her, but if I'm left to wonder about the details, not knowing will drive me up the wall." She wiggled to sit within the reassuring curve of his arm. "It's a lot of information to take in all at once."

"I was thinking that the diary might hold a clue about who might be setting these fires."

She turned to look into his eyes. "I don't see how. It's about my mother's life, not mine. Mom didn't even start it until she got pregnant."

"But, that's the point. If we're right, someone is very angry with you, but we don't know why. It may not be something recent. It might have something to do with a misunderstanding from years ago."

"How long can one person hold a grudge? And how could I have done something terrible as a child and not even remember it?"

Aaron thought about all of the tragedy caused by anger he'd been witness to in his jobs. "Oh, you'd be surprised about people and their grudges. The arsonist's actions demonstrate a lot of bottled-up hate. What if it's gone on for years?" His mind milled with all the possibilities. "Maybe you weren't paranoid about those other two fires."

"I just can't imagine what I've done to earn that kind of response from anyone. I know I'm not perfect, but—"

The guilt he heard in her voice shocked him. "None of this is your fault. I didn't mean to imply that at all."

"How do you know?"

"Because things like this aren't based on sound reasoning. I'd bet the real motivation behind these fires is going to perplex us, because this guy's mental process is probably as out of whack as his recent actions seem to dictate."

"What if it's a woman?"

"Well, anything is possible, I guess, but female arsonists are quite rare, so it's not likely."

"I didn't know that. How rare?"

"Ten to eighteen percent, depending on the study. So, the odds are that ours is likely a male. Statistically, most arsonists are young, under-employed men. I also don't think most women would take a chance with a child's life."

"What do you mean?"

He realized that, with all the fuss, he hadn't told her about the latest fire. It took a few minutes to fill her in on the details. "We don't know if he knew the child was there or not. According to Ty, the parents are very unreliable. But if he set it knowing the child was there, he's accelerating."

"All this drama makes my head hurt." Squeezing her tight, he changed the subject, not wanting to add to her growing list of worries. But one thing occurred to him. If the current fires were linked to the other two fires she'd been in, then the arsonist might be much older than they had considered until now. It was time to shift the whole focus of these crimes and consider a totally different type of suspect.

## Chapter Twelve

The next morning, as soon as Aaron reached the station, he made a call to Ty and told him about John Sutton. He tried not to make the request personal, but it sure felt that way. He didn't want the older man anywhere near Harper.

"You want me to check him out for you?"

"I'd appreciate it. It just seems like strange timing to me that her old beau shows up out of nowhere, right in the midst of these fires. And she seemed surprised that he found himself at such a small school. I'm wondering if he chose that position because he already knew she lived nearby."

"Sounds like this guy is a lot older than her."

"A lot older; almost twice her age. She referred to him as her one and only age-gap mistake."

"That should make you feel better."

"I'd feel a lot happier if he would go away and leave us in peace. I don't need any more distractions."

"This guy's worth looking into, considering we don't have anything else. He may just want a second chance with her, though."

"Never going to happen." His words had a more strident tone than he'd intended.

Ty laughed. "That sounds pretty territorial to me. You getting serious about settling down, old man?"

"You bet. Let's just hope she's starting to feel the

same way." Time to change the subject. "Did you find out anything else about Arne's gambling debts?"

"A source told us he paid down part of the debt with some money from his retirement fund. Stupid fool. We couldn't find anything that seemed to show that he paid anyone to set the fire."

"So, another dead end."

"As far as I can tell. At least we can rule him out. We'll keep looking. Sooner or later, we're going to figure this out." They signed off and Aaron got back to the endless stack of paperwork. As he was wrapping it up, an old friend from the state fire authorities called to tell him that Ira Johnson had called and tried to lodge a formal complaint against him.

*Just what I need right now, on top of everything else.* "Oh, for heaven's sake, I just looked at his fire to see if it had anything in common with mine. His former assistant accompanied me. The chief couldn't be reached by phone which, apparently, is a common problem over there."

The other man swore under his breath. "Oh, don't worry, we know exactly how bad of a job he's doing. Keep it between you and me, but there's going to be a quiet investigation because there's been so many complaints about him over the last few months. Not just from other firemen, either. A lot are from people in his own town." He gave a dramatic groan. "I was just calling to make you aware and tell you not to worry about it. The powers-that-be informed him that he doesn't have a leg to stand on. They said he should get back to work and worry about his own station."

Thanking him for the warning, he hung up and mulled over the problem. How on earth had such an inept man not been fired already? As if he didn't have his hands full already with an arsonist on the loose and a persistent ex-boyfriend to check out. Once he gave it some thought, he called Rocky into his office. He joined him at once, his eyes inquisitive. "What's up, Aaron?"

"I'd like you to write down exactly what happened the day you got fired, so that we have it on file. Chief Johnson is making waves. We can deal with it, but I want to have everything on file for our own protection."

"Yes, Chief. Sorry about all the fuss."

"Nobody's fault but his own. It's a good lesson though, to have a complete record in order to protect yourself. It's just been so hectic around here, I forgot." He met the other man's gaze. "Can't really trust our memories in case we have to make a statement sometime in the future."

"I'll do it right now, while it's quiet." Nodding, he left the room. Twenty minutes later, he brought the statement back and Aaron filed it in case he ever needed it.

When he was caught up on his other items, he called Jim into the office and waved him to a seat. "Do you remember Harper's mom? I know you and she would have been about the same age now had she lived."

"Sure," he nodded, smiling. "We went to school together. She was real pretty and friendly. Damn shame the cancer took her so young."

"Did you know her father?"

"Not as much. He went to school in Springvale, so he wasn't really part of our regular crowd. Everyone was a little surprised when the two of them got married."

"Why is that?"

"He was a real quiet guy, studious, and she was

always the life of the party. Not in a bad way, you understand. She just liked to laugh and have fun." He shrugged. "They married too young, I think. Those things never seem to last."

"Did you ever date her?"

He shook his head, kicking the toe of his boot against the chair leg. "Nah, but not for lack of trying. I asked her out and she let me down gently." Looking up, he grinned. "Better than getting slammed down, I guess."

"You remember anyone else who dated her or wanted to? Anyone who was especially persistent?" He didn't mention the letter J, in case it distracted him.

"I know just about every guy around tried, but she was picky. She'd always use that old standby. You know, let's just be friends." He shrugged. "At least she said it with a smile." His gaze met his own. "Why, was Harper asking about her momma?"

He didn't want to share information that wasn't his, so he replied, "She's just curious about her life, I guess. Her mom died so young and she knows very little about her personal history."

"I can understand that."

"If you remember anything else, will you let me know?"

"Of course." He shut the door behind him, leaving Aaron to his circling thoughts.

After going back and forth considering the wisdom of it, he called his mother. Her voice, as always, cheered him. "I have a strange question for you, mom. Harper found an old diary of her mother's and in it, she refers to someone called J. Not the name, just the initial. It's probably for a first name. Does anyone spring to mind?"

"Well, June Claiborne jumps to mind, I guess."

"Sorry, I should have clarified. It would have been a man, someone around your age."

"You mean someone as young as me?" She laughed at her own joke.

Her teasing made him smile. "Yes, about that young." She gave him four or five names and he wrote them down on his pad.

"Who knew J was such a popular initial?" She hummed. "They're the only ones I can think of, honey."

"Okay, thanks."

"Are you going to tell me what all this is about?"

"I'd have to check with Harper first. She's pretty private."

"Oh, that's fine. I don't want you to get in any trouble." When he went to sign off, she spoke again. "I really like her, by the way."

"So do I."

"Is she going to stick around for a while? Not a bad idea to keep her close by if you can."

Her advice made him grin. "If I have anything to say about it, she won't be going anywhere. Will that do for now?"

"That's enough to make me smile. Talk to you soon. Love you." Hanging up, he got back to work.

That evening, he and Harper had decided to grab a burger for dinner because they were too tired to cook. Having just pushed her chair in behind her at Pete's, he had taken a seat when a tall, blond man strode over from across the room. Before she spoke, he already had a suspicion who he was. "John, what are you doing here?" The tips of her ears turned pink as she looked uneasily at him.

His eyes roamed her body and Aaron gritted his

teeth. "Just grabbing some dinner, same as you. And who is this?" Raising his eyebrows, he glanced across the table.

He rose to his feet, towering over the creep. "Aaron Lassiter. And you are…?"

"Dr. John Sutton."

Not surprising he felt compelled to add the doctor label. Aaron smiled. "Oh, Harper's old pal from school." The subtle stress on the old didn't escape the other man's attention, judging by him straightening to meet his gaze. As she'd mentioned, he looked a lot older than her and what his mother would call a little too slick for his own good.

His smile dimmed, then changed to a smirk, making him look even more like a weasel. "Oh, we were much more than friends." He said the taunting words, clearly hoping to both surprise and annoy him.

Leaning down, Aaron brushed a hand over Harper's shining hair. "Well, that's old, long-buried history, now, isn't it?"

"I don't know, is it?"

Harper paled. "John, I think—"

Sutton didn't even pretend to listen to her. Puffing out his chest, he said, "I never thought she would settle for a blue-collar man like you. You're not exactly her usual type, you know."

"He is now." Apparently, Harper had decided she'd had enough. Her brows were drawn together, her jaw tilted up. Aaron almost smiled at the righteous anger lighting her eyes. "I think it's time you move on. We're trying to enjoy our dinner and I made myself clear about my wishes the other day." Her defiant response warmed him.

Sutton gave a mocking bow. "As you wish, my dear. You know where to find me when inevitable boredom sets in. And it will." Strolling back to the opposite table, he dropped some bills on its surface and exited, his arrogant strut gaining attention. The curious gazes of the other diners bounced back and forth between them.

He sat as an awkward silence settled over the table. "I'm so sorry," Harper whispered, her eyes downcast.

Aaron reached across the table to let his fingers stroke her closest hand. "Why are you sorry? You did nothing wrong. I must say, though, it's obvious your taste in men has recently improved a lot." The feeble attempt to make her smile failed.

She looked close to tears. "He shouldn't be so disrespectful of you. It makes me sick."

Patting her arm, he said, "Oh, honey, if I worried about what men like him had to say, I would have been eaten alive years ago. You have to laugh, really. He doesn't have much to stand on besides his pile of degrees, does he?"

She shook her head. "Still, I would have hoped childish behavior like that was beneath him."

"What made him attractive enough for you to date? Beyond his looks, I mean. I'm just curious."

After a long sigh, she said, "I was both lonely and naïve. I thought his intelligence and maturity would make him good company, but he spent most of our time together talking about himself. It was a major education on the type of man I should avoid dating."

"That doesn't surprise me, but he seems to be under the impression he still has a chance with you."

"There's no way in hell I'd ever date him again. I learned my lesson the hard way." She peeked through her lashes, conjuring a smile out of nowhere. "Besides, I have much better company these days."

Relief loosened the muscles in his shoulders. "Glad to hear you think so."

She leaned forward to whisper, "Maybe we should introduce him to Stacy and get rid of two problems at once."

"That's a great idea." He glanced around and waved at the waitress. "After our burgers, why don't we celebrate that with a big piece of pie?"

"Make that chocolate cake and you've got a deal."

\*\*\*\*

Late the next day, Harper paged through the diary, absorbing her mother's increasingly worried words. Her ex-lover, the mysterious J, had started phoning her at all hours and leaving her written messages in odd places all over the property. His threats ran from telling her husband to spreading lies about Harper's parentage. At least her mother's comments were specific enough to put one thing to rest—she was, indeed, born of the man she'd always known as her father. Her mother's recounting of J's bitter comments made that as clear as glass. A huge wave of relief swamped her, then she continued.

The diary read: *His tormenting behavior seems endless and the strain is taking a toll on my marriage. I look at Harper's innocent face and pray she never makes a mistake with men that she will pay for until eternity. J appeared to be the perfect man, educated and sophisticated, and look how that turned out. I was a gullible fool. I ruined everything.*

*It doesn't help that I haven't been feeling well lately. My energy is half of what it used to be. My baby's smiling face is the only thing that keeps me going. Something's wrong with me.*

Harper's eyes backtracked a few lines. *Educated.* That was the first real clue about his identity, other than the letter J. So, he was probably a white-collar worker. The clue excited her. It was a fairly small town, even smaller back in those years. With his initial, and now this snippet of information, she could certainly at least narrow the field.

Thinking about professional occupations, she wrote a list: lawyers, doctors, engineers… She couldn't wait to tell Aaron about his latest development.

Chapter Thirteen

After a long, busy day at the station the next day, Aaron was just closing things down for the day when his cell phone rang. Tempted not to answer it, he changed his mind when he saw it was Ty on the other end. He punched the answer button. "What's up? I was just about to head home."

"Thought I'd try to catch you before you were around Harper. I got the report on the ex-boyfriend and wasn't too sure you'd told her that you're looking into him."

"I didn't see any point in upsetting her. She's had enough to deal with lately. Did you find out anything interesting?"

"A few things that might make us want to keep an eye on him."

"Oh, really?" He felt a surge of guilty interest. He wasn't sure Harper would approve of his actions, but he wasn't taking any chances with her safety.

"Yup. Apparently, he lost his job at Harper's alma mater because of numerous complaints of aggressive behavior toward women. The jerk doesn't seem to know the meaning of the word no. He kept phoning, sending emails, etcetera, long after two different women turned him down."

"Doesn't surprise me."

"No, but this might. When he was an undergrad, his

dormitory burnt down, and they looked pretty hard at him for arson. He'd been chastised by the house manager earlier that day and didn't take it very well."

Now, that bit of news he wasn't expecting. "I'd say that's certainly worth a second look."

"I agree, but supposedly no evidence could be found and they had to let it drop. And it was so long ago, I doubt we'll find anyone that remembers the case." He blew a snort of frustration. "He threatened the head honcho, saying he'd get his, but then told the authorities he was just blowing hot air. They were forced to believe him, because they had nothing that proved otherwise. Still, it's enough to make you wonder."

"What is his last university going to do about his behavior toward women?"

"They kept it hush-hush and agreed to back off if he left the university. From what my source told me, that's pretty common behavior for universities. They don't want any bad press."

"Nothing like passing the problem teacher onto the next bunch. Why wouldn't the community college find out about his transgressions when they did their search?"

"They likely did a cursory check, because they were so glad to have someone of his expertise."

He cursed. "Dammit, that's how these bastards get away with things like that."

"Don't worry. I've got a friend who teaches over there. I'll put a bug in her ear and she'll keep an eye out and make sure he minds his manners." He laughed. "She's fearless. I wouldn't want to get on her bad side."

"Okay, well, that helps. In the meantime, I'll see if I can dig up anyone who knows anything about the dorm fire."

"That'll work. Let me know if you find anything." Happy to be done for the day, Aaron headed home.

**\*\*\*\***

Aaron and Harper discussed her new clue over dinner. Now, it seemed like he was chasing snowflakes, what with all the snippets of information they were gathering. He had responded by telling her what he'd learned about Sutton. "I wish I could say I'm surprised," she said, looking disgusted. "He's not used to being turned down and it's probably happening more often, now that he's older. It's funny, I don't remember him mentioning anything about him being in a fire, but I guess it's not exactly something you'd broadcast, is it?"

"No, you certainly wouldn't, especially if he was questioned about it. Whether he's a suspect or not, if he becomes a pest, I want to know at once. He doesn't seem to think he should back off just because you're in a relationship. That lack of respect bothers me."

She poked him in the belly. "What, are you going to do, play Neanderthal and beat on your chest to scare him off?"

"If it comes to that." She might be teasing, but he meant every word.

"Interesting. You know, I'm an independent woman who can take care of herself, but still, that territorial stuff is kinda sexy." Grunting to make her laugh, he picked her up and carried her to bed.

Hours later, he lay, wide awake, in bed as she slept, thinking about his conversation with Jim. Mentioning it to Harper seemed inappropriate, somehow, so he kept it to himself for now. He ran over every word they'd exchanged, sighing when he realized none of what the other man had said helped in their search. Then, a disturbing thought invaded his brain. Jim was about the same age as Harper's mother, had known and wanted her. And Aaron knew something important that the others didn't. Before he became a fireman, Jim had been a chemist. Anybody would consider that a professional, white-collar job. So, he was the right age, a former professional, and his name started with J. It couldn't be him, it just couldn't be. Jim was the backbone of the station, his trusted right hand. But, as his thoughts ran around and around in a dazed circle, he realized he would have to check his good friend out, regardless of his personal bias.

**** 

The next day, Harper showed up early for her appointment at the hospital. Today was the big day. She would get her cast off for good, as long as the x-ray showed it had healed properly. A new technician led her through the process and removed it for her. Underneath the cast, her arm looked shriveled and pale, the muscles weak and slightly sore from having been so long out of use. Dr. Mason popped in, looking distracted. "Your x-ray looks fine. Harry will take you down to the physiotherapy department so you can set up appointments. Three times a week for a month should help restore your strength and flexibility."

"Thank you." Nodding, he left as quickly as he'd come. Her appointments were booked easily. She preferred to come in the early mornings when it was quieter. Aaron left early for work, so she was up anyway. When she checked the area out, she thought all of the machines certainly looked intriguing, not at all like the torture devices she'd envisioned. The equipment looked more like what you'd find at a small playground.

After she was finished at the hospital, she went for a stroll down Main Street. She'd been cooped up for so long she missed the simple enjoyment of daily life. Waving hello to a few people who passed, she window-shopped until her stomach rumbled and checking her watch, she was shocked to find it was lunch time already. As she paused to consider her options, a big, burly man came to a halt in front of her. Towering over her, he stared, his dark eyes glowing with hatred. Disturbed, she took a step back and went to move around him. More worried when he moved a step to the side to block her progress, she said "Can I help you?" in the frostiest tone she could manage.

"Damn right, you can. You can start by telling your man to stay the hell out of my business." She smelt his chewing tobacco and he paused to spit a tainted puddle down beside her feet.

Cringing with disgust, she said, "I don't even know who you are." When she tried once again to pass him, he trapped her good wrist with one meaty paw. "Let me go!"

"Harper, do you need help?" The woman's voice floated from somewhere behind her. In desperation, she turned a few degrees and spied Sandra hurrying up to her. Relief flushed through her. Ty's wife seemed to assess the situation at once. "Chief Johnson, you need to release her right now."

Scowling, he did, dropping her hand like a dirty rag. "Your men need to take care of your town and leave Springvale to me. The bunch of ya just need to mind your own damn business." He looked them both up and down, leering, before centering his look on Harper's face once again. "You're a troublemaker, just like your mother.

Neither one of ya could recognize a good man to save your lives." Turning on his heel, he stomped away, muttering curses under his breath.

"Are you okay?" The concern on Sandra's face warmed her. "That ignorant bully didn't do anything else, did he?"

"N-no." She huffed a breath to calm herself. "I didn't even know who he was, but he seemed to think I should recognize him."

"He's the fire chief over in Springvale." Sandra lowered her voice, checking around for eavesdroppers. "Our men have been digging a little into the fires in his precinct and he seems quite resentful. We'll have to tell them about this."

"I don't want any more trouble. We have enough to deal with."

Sandra shook her head. "He grabbed you, Harper. That's not okay. Thank goodness it wasn't your injured hand, at least." She squeezed her shoulder. "I was just headed to the hospital to see if you'd gotten the cast off, but I see I'm too late for the grand unveiling." Bending, she took a closer look. "It looks a little wimpy now, but it will be up to snuff in no time."

"I hope so. They gave me some exercises to help and made appointments for me with the physiotherapy department." Finally, her body stopped shaking. "I was going to stop for lunch before—"

"Well, perfect timing then. It's ladies lunch day at Pete's. My treat." She linked arms with her and led the way.

Harper felt better once they were both safely inside and settled in a booth. She sipped a glass of ice water as she tried to decide what to eat. Sandra sent a text and then did the same. In the end, they decided they deserved a treat and both chose chicken tenders, fries and a milkshake. They had chatted for ten minutes when, suddenly, the front door flew open and Ty entered with Aaron right behind him. Looking like gunslingers about to fire a few rounds, they stood braced while they scanned the room.

"Oh, for goodness' sake," Sandra muttered. "Here comes our personal security team."

"Are you both okay?" The men said it in harmony as if they'd practiced, striding over to stand beside them.

"We're fine," Sandra said before Harper could say a word. "I just texted you so you'd be aware of what happened. You didn't have to come racing over here."

They wiggled over to make room for them on the bench seats. Aaron stroked her hair as the other two whispered. "Are you sure he didn't hurt you?"

Harper nodded. "It was just confusing. I didn't even know who he was, but he seemed to think I should."

"Sandra said he grabbed you by the wrist. Which one?"

"The healthy one, thank goodness." He lifted it and saw where a bruise was blooming. "Son of a—"

"It's okay. I just bruise easily. As soon as Sandra joined us, he backed off."

"I'm just glad she was close by." He took a deep breath, letting it back out slowly. She knew it was his way of trying to calm himself. "What exactly did he say to you?"

"That you guys should mind your own business and stay in your own town. And he said something about me being a troublemaker just like my mother."

The two man's gazes met and what she saw in their

expressions made her shiver. Aaron's expression softened again when he turned back to her. "We'll take care of it."

Ty said, "You two come to the station and file a report when you're finished lunch, okay?"

At first, Harper tried to talk them out of it, but Ty pointed out that he might hurt someone worse the next time he lost his temper. After thinking about it, she agreed. Aaron asked, "Can you drive Harper home afterward, Sandra?"

"Of course." The men filed back through the door as efficiently as they'd arrived. Sandra watched them, shaking her head. "I love having a protective man, but sometimes, they need to trust that we can take care of a difficult situation."

"It's all pretty new to me, having someone who cares so much." Harper could feel her cheeks turning red as the other diners glanced her way.

"Well, I'd guess they'll make certain that Ira regrets his behavior, that's for sure." She rubbed her hands together. "Here comes the food. Let's dig in. We can worry about the rest of this nonsense after we eat."

She was right—eating calmed them both. Afterward, filling out the report at the sheriff's department only took thirty minutes and then Sandra dropped her off at home. As she entered the house, waving goodbye to her friend, she realized that's exactly how she thought of this place. Home. There was nothing definite about their future—especially right now—and she wondered if she was getting too attached. She pushed the troubling thought away. They had enough problems to deal with right now.

After Aaron got home and they'd eaten dinner, she

noticed that he was quieter than normal. "Is something wrong? You seem a little off tonight."

Rubbing his face, he plopped down on the sofa and she joined him. "Everything is just really complicated right now. Lately, it seems like everywhere I turn, I find another potential for who J is."

"Who are you thinking about?"

"Well, there's your ex-boyfriend, for one. John."

She laughed. "You're getting carried away because you don't like him. He didn't even know my mom."

"How do you know? He's a lot older than you. And did you know he grew up just a few towns away?"

It surprised her that he hadn't mentioned that. "It's true—I didn't know that. I still think that's stretching things a bit. Who else is on the list?"

"Jim, from the station."

Now she understood why he seemed sad. "Oh, that can't be right. He's wonderful. I could never see him being wrapped up in this mess."

"He knew your mother. He even asked her out once and she turned him down."

"So did a lot of people. And besides, I'm not sure my mother would consider a fireman a professional, no offense."

He told her about Jim's past as a chemist.

She shook her head. "I still don't see it. He's been wonderful to me from day one. He'd have to be a fabulous actor to fake that."

"I hope you're right."

"Is that it, then? Just the two of them as serious possibilities?"

"I thought so until today."

A sudden shiver caused her to pause and pull a

blanket over her legs. "What happened today?"

"I guess after you guys filled out your report, one of Ty's older deputies made a comment about Ira being sweet on your mom at one time. Apparently, they dated for a while and only broke up after he started drinking too much."

A shiver chased down her back. "I hate the thought of her being anywhere close to that guy. I guess that's why he made that remark about her not being able to recognize a good man. Sour grapes."

"Seems hard to believe she'd ever be interested, but I guess he wasn't always that way. Before he drank so much, I guess he was a decent guy or so the locals tell me. And a lot of men don't deal well with rejection."

"But would a man who saves lives for a living ever put them in jeopardy? It seems like a stretch to believe that would happen."

Aaron nodded. "There have been cases of fireman turning to the dark side, but that's mostly when they set fires and then race in to put them out again. They call it Savior Syndrome. We all get a rush out of saving people, but they take it a step further and create the problem, then solve it."

"I don't blame you for feeling exhausted. It's all so frustrating. What are you going to do?"

"I don't just have those three, I have a dozen more who meet our parameters and the list keeps growing." He leaned against the back of the couch, closing his eyes. "I'll try my best to rule them out, one by one."

\*\*\*\*

Harper was hard at work in the barn the next morning when a lengthy shadow filled the doorway. She looked up, hoping to see Aaron. Instead, she found the last person she wanted to see—John leaning against the frame, looking smug. "Well, isn't this quaint?" Now that she'd caught sight of him, he strolled inside without waiting for an invitation. Glancing around, he gave a derisive snort.

Struggling to keep hold of her temper, she said, "What are you doing here? Shouldn't you be at work?"

He shrugged. "That's the virtue of being a big fish in a little pond. They let you do damn near anything you please, as long as you teach a few classes."

Him being here on Aaron's property made her uncomfortable and she stood so she'd feel less vulnerable. How many times did she have to say no to this jerk? Not for the first time, she cursed the precious time she'd wasted on him. To feel safe, she kept the hammer she'd been using in her hand. "I think we covered everything that needs to be said the other night."

"Oh, did we?" He smirked at her latest piece of furniture as if such workmanship was beneath him. "I learned something interesting yesterday. A little birdie told me that you wouldn't even date the Chief until after the fire. You turned him down until he had a hand in saving you."

"That's none of your business."

Ignoring her, he tilted his head, his gaze meeting hers. "Why is that, Harper? And did it ever occur to you that he might have set the house on fire himself just to get close to you?"

His ridiculous ploy to make her doubt herself made her laugh loud. "Now, you're really reaching. But I'll be sure to tell him what you said. People get sued for saying less provocative things than that." She smiled, just to irritate him. "By the way, I found out why you got kicked out of our old university. I can't say the complaints from several different women surprised me."

His gaze narrowed. "That was a little misunderstanding."

"One of many, apparently. Funny how these misunderstandings tend to follow you around, isn't it?"

"Poor oversensitive Harper." He sneered. "You wouldn't be so uptight if you'd learned how to share a desirable man like me. You always did blow things out of proportion."

"So says every abuser in the universe." She dusted her hands off and gestured to the door, all of her polite instincts long gone. "It's time for you to leave. You shouldn't be on Aaron's property without his permission."

"What—you're not referring to it as ours yet? You seem more than ready to lay claim to whatever's his." Pausing in front of her, he said, "If your man's such a winner, then why hasn't he caught this arsonist?"

"Oh, he will, sooner than you think."

His face reddened and his fists clenched. Suddenly, she recognized the less attractive version of the man she'd finally seen at the end of their relationship. "You seem so confident about that, yet the evidence seems to point to a pathetic failure on his part. He doesn't seem to have the brain power to figure out what's really going on."

She reined in the surge of temper that made her want to fly to Aaron's defense. Men like John always wanted women to lose control, so he could claim instability on their part. She refused to fall into that trap. Her next words had a distinct chill to prove that point. "He'll always be ten times the man you are without even trying.

And everyone in the town will cheer him when he does solve the case. In the meantime, get out and don't come back."

He chuckled and turned to leave. Watching him saunter back to his car made her want to kick him in the butt to get him moving. He took his sweet time as if he could read her thoughts. As he drove away in his fancy black car, she had a thought. Had it been him she saw cruising by the other day? There was no way to know for sure.

It would have been nice to keep his visit to herself, but it felt wrong not to tell Aaron. That evening, she filled him in about John's visit as they ate dinner and she didn't miss the storm cloud expression that followed. "Don't worry. I took care of it," she said to reassure him. "I just thought you should know since it's your property."

"I'm not worried about my property, I'm concerned about you. He wouldn't dare come here if I was around." She saw him tense up, his biceps flexing, and knew he wished he could punch him.

"That's true." In a way, she was grateful he hadn't been around, because it really might have come to blows. He was disciplined with his temper, but everyone had a breaking point. Neither one of them needed another distraction. She decided not to mention her question about whether he'd driven by before. It didn't really matter at this point.

To change the subject, she mentioned what she'd found in the diary excerpt she'd read while waiting for dinner to cook. "There's a mention of two small local fires that they suspected might be arson. That would have been about thirty years ago." She met his gaze. "My mother wrote that when she mentioned them, J smiled and didn't seem at all concerned. His reaction bothered her."

His eyes lit. "If her instincts were right, we might actually have a chance at catching him. We need to knuckle down on the information in that diary."

Chapter Fourteen

At the station the next morning, Aaron made time for another chat with Jim. His worries about what the arsonist had planned next pestered him all night. A nagging feeling persisted that, if they could just put all these tiny pieces together, they would create a detailed picture. After shutting the office door behind him, Jim grabbed a coffee from the nearby coffeepot and took a seat. Grinning, he said, "I don't know if it's a good or bad thing to be called into the boss's office two days in a row."

Aaron felt guilty, measuring every word the other man said as he looked for answers, but there was no way around it. "Nothing's wrong. I really just wanted your impressions of this case. You've been a firefighter for a long while now. Is there any angle we could pursue that I haven't thought of?"

His relaxed demeanor never faltered as he slouched back in his chair, taking a sip of coffee. "I think you're doing everything you can. Even though the statistics say it's likely a teenager, I agree with your analysis. I don't think that's what we're dealing with here. The whole case seems atypical, which makes finding any helpful clues even more difficult."

"I don't understand why Harper is a target. If we could figure out the motivation behind the fire at her rental, I think we'll have the key to catching him."

The other man's face revealed nothing. "It could be that we're wrong about her being a target. Maybe she was just in the wrong place at the wrong time."

"I wish that were true, but I don't think it's likely. With her being hit on the head like that, it certainly seems personal to me."

"Have to agree with you there. I was trying to play the devil's advocate. The simplest answer is usually the correct one."

"There's nothing simple about this case, I'm afraid." He took a drink of coffee. "Are you still planning to retire next year?"

"I think so. My poor ol' bones hurt a lot more than they used to and I've put off a lot of fishing trips until now." He met his gaze. "Are you grooming Rocky to take my place?"

"It's too early to know for sure. We'll see how he does in the meantime. How do you think the others will react if I decide to do that?"

"Given enough time for them to get to know him, I don't think it will be a problem. Most of the others aren't interested in heading the ranks. They like more regular hours and most have families to get home to." He grinned. "Looks like you might be headed in that direction yourself with that girl of yours, am I right?"

"We've been spending a lot of time together. Just between you and me, I have hopes in that direction." He struggled to sound casual. "You like Harper, don't you?"

"What's not to like? She makes you happy and she brings us baked goods all the time. That's a win/win as far as I'm concerned." He stood, stretching. "Are we done for now? I have that fire education seminar at the high school. I need to head out in a few minutes."

"Of course. You'll let me know if you have any other ideas about these fires?"

"Sure thing." As Jim left. It occurred to him that, once again, he hadn't learned a damn thing that would ease the stewing worry in his gut.

Mid-afternoon, Aaron took a break and decided to pay his adversary a visit. He waited beside Sutton's car in the university parking lot in Springvale. Having checked his schedule at the head office, he'd found out that his last class let out a few minutes ago. The secretary, an old friend from high school, told him he normally left immediately after classes ended for the day. He decided to wait outside, so as not to cause any undue attention. He watched, feeling ancient in comparison, as students streamed down the various paths nearby, chatting and laughing. As predicted, he caught sight of Sutton exiting the front door, a leather briefcase in one hand. His steps slowed as he grew closer, checking him out with an adolescent smirk. "Well, if it isn't Harper's blue-collar boyfriend. What are you doing here? Trying to gather a few extra brain cells?"

Aaron ignored the childish taunt. "I'm making certain you receive a very clear message." He waited until the other man came to a stop, then stepped forward, using his greater height to his advantage. "Stay away from my home and my girlfriend. She has made it more than clear, several times, that she's not interested in your company."

He ran a hand through his hair, grinning. "Maybe you're hoping that if you repeat it enough, it will be true."

Continuing as if the idiot hadn't spoken, he said, "If you approach her again, I'll report you for trespassing and harassment. And with your other issues from your last workplace, I'm willing to bet neither your reputation nor your career will survive."

His face flushed, his teeth clenched. He didn't look so suave and cocksure anymore. "Get the hell away from me." Aaron stepped back and watched as the other man yanked open the door, then threw his case on the passenger side seat. He kept his eyes on him as he started the car, backed up and zoomed away.

Well, at least he'd accomplished one thing today. That should take care of the little weasel. He whistled as he got into his truck and drove away.

****

Getting desperate to gain Aaron's attention, Stacy came up with what she thought was a foolproof plan to finally snare him. First, she confirmed that he was working at the station later than normal. Knowing the firehouse was short-handed, she made a simple phone call that confirmed his delay in getting home. She didn't know where that bitch Harper was, but all the lights in both houses were off and her truck was gone when she checked. So, once she'd dressed to impress, she drove back over to his place, hiding her car so it was out of sight. She wore a long wool coat over the special lingerie she's purchased just to please him, giggling with delight over her daring plan. The extra effort wouldn't be wasted on him. He was more than worth the cost. She scolded herself for not thinking of doing this before now.

She found the heavy, wooden front door locked, no big surprise, but she didn't want to actually break any glass. Luckily, she found a window in back that he hadn't secured. She gave the wood frame a small push, delighted when it edged up a few inches. Laughing when she peeked in, she saw it was to obviously his bedroom, her intended destination. Surely that was a sign from the passion gods, she thought with a grin.

Using a small branch, she wedged the stubborn window open the eighteen inches that she needed. Hopping up, she slithered through the opening, careful not to rip her clothing. Closing the window behind her to keep the cold night air out, she peeled off the coat and laid it over a nearby chair. She pulled her outfit carefully into place before arranging herself artfully on the bed. Plumping her breasts to show their lush bounty had her remembering with a giggle that another man had paid for them. As the boring minutes ticked by, she made herself more comfortable against the pillows. She didn't know how much longer Aaron would be at the station, but his muscular body guaranteed he would certainly be worth the wait. And if that bitch showed up instead, she could convince her that he had just left after satisfying her. Picturing that dramatic scene in her imagination made her smile and led her to doze off.

The creaking floor in the hallway woke her with a start a short while later. Heavy steps told her it had to be a man. Fluffing her hair, she felt her heart racing in anticipation as the sounds grew closer. She stretched out, so the first thing he would see were her long, tanned legs, her best attribute. As the door swung open with a small squeak, she put on her sexiest smile, pursing her ruby lips. But the person who entered the room wasn't Aaron or even Harper. Confusion caused her to gasp. "What are you doing here?"

Dr. Mason paused, his head tilting to one side as he took in the sight of her from her legs all the way up to, finally, her eyes. "I could ask you the same thing, Stacy."

She'd taken him for a joyride once or twice, just for kicks. He was pretty insatiable for an old guy. "I thought I'd hang around and give Aaron a sexy surprise." Preening, she said, "What do you think?"

He paused to glance around the room. "I think he's pretty involved with Harper, isn't he? Don't you think you're intruding where you're not wanted?" He met her gaze once again, moving a step closer, and she saw a rare, passionate intent in his usually ice gray eyes.

"It's past time he left that boring bitch behind." Pouting, she shoved against the heavy, wooden headboard, wiggling to sit up. "What's that smell?" Sniffing, she stared at him. "You smell like gasoline."

"Do I? How very strange."

Premonition darted up her back like a poisonous insect. With a clutch of sudden fear, she noticed he wore gloves and stuttered, "W-what are you doing? Why do you have gloves on?"

"I have some personal business to take care of and I'm afraid you're in my way."

She shrank away from him, fear rocketing through her. "Whaddya mean?" Too late, her breath gushed out in a pant and a latent need to flee grabbed ahold. Her heels dug for purchase against the slick surface of the bed linens. "N-never mind. I'll just go." Searching for an exit, she realized he stood between her and the door. She'd never raise the window in time.

"I'm afraid, my dear, that you're what I might refer to as collateral damage." Lunging forward, he grabbed her around the throat, shoving her back onto the mattress. She tried to strike out at him to no avail. He squeezed as she fought him, his towering strength insurmountable.

As her vision dimmed, her last bizarre thought was that the expensive lingerie would be wasted after all.

## Chapter Fifteen

Harper drove toward home, exhaustion creeping into her limbs. Her hand ached and her feet were falling asleep from her having driven for so long. *What a wasted day.* The farmer who had promised her all the beautiful old lumber from his vintage barn had reneged on his promise to sell it to her at the agreed price. His idiot son had convinced him to double the asking price, putting it well out of her price range. All she had to show for her day's work was an unnecessary gasoline bill and an empty stomach from missing lunch. She wanted a hot shower, food, and Aaron, in that order, as soon as possible.

As she drew close to home, an unusual orange light through the trees caught her eye, the color stark against the darkness surrounding it. Taking her foot off the gas pedal, she stared in confusion. Her system finally registered that it wasn't a flickering light that came from the side of Aaron's house. It was flames, the edges growing out of control as she watched. She yanked her truck to the side of the road, skidding to a stop, and grabbed her cellphone from her purse. When the emergency operator answered, she sputtered, "It's Harper. There's a fire at the chief's house on Blackman Road. Send everyone."

Hanging up, she sped up the drive to her cottage, scattering the gravel as she came to an abrupt stop and threw it in park. Leaving the truck there for safety, she raced back down the hill. Near the back patio was a hose Aaron kept connected to the outdoor faucet. Grabbing it, she turned it on full blast and aimed at his bedroom window where the flames flared out. The heat blasted in her face, a sickening shock after the chill. There was no way to tell how far the fire had spread inside. After an agonizing three or four minutes, the shriek of sirens called to her from down the road. She forced her exhausted arms to keep at it, hoping her efforts might save the rest of the house. Soaking the exterior and what she could reach of the roof, she heard a firetruck hustle up the drive followed by other vehicles. A minute or two later, she heard someone bellow, "Harper," over the roar of the flames and knew it had to be Aaron.

"Back here," she yelled as the men came at a run. Two of them stabilized a much larger hose and aimed it at the roof. With their masks on, she couldn't tell one from the other. Strong arms pulled her away from the flames and Aaron cradled her in his arms. When she looked up at him, she saw his fear for her in the drawn muscles of his face.

"Are you okay?"

She caught her breath, panting, "Yes, I'm fine. Just a little shaky."

"Tell me what happened." He brushed her hair out of her face, his eyes somber.

Sucking in another breath, she said, "I don't know. I was almost home before I saw the flames coming out of your bedroom window. I just pulled over and called for help."

He nodded and stared into her eyes. "You've done your bit. Now I need you to stand well back and let us work."

"Okay." More than happy to do as he asked, she watched him organizing the others and barking orders as she went to sit cross-legged on a stretch of nearby lawn. Ignoring her trembling limbs, she tried to calm down and get her panicked breathing back to normal. Ignoring her aching wrist, she realized she'd never seen the men at work before now. They knew what they were doing—she had faith that they would put it out.

Men ran back and forth, shouting and switching off to preserve energy. The flames finally began to subside. She struggled not to cry at the sight of the jagged, gaping hole in the side of his house. By some miracle, it didn't appear to have reached the upper floor or the kitchen, but she could tell both downstairs bedrooms were gone by the blackened windows. An odd, rank odor reached her as she waited and she wrinkled her nose, finally covering her nostrils with her bent arm. Whatever it was made her stomach heave and she didn't want to get sick. It would only worry Aaron even more.

Someone called, "Chief! We need you in here," his voice tense. After a few moments of relative quiet, people started hustling back and forth, their faces somber. When she called out to ask what was going on, no one answered. She wondered what could possibly have gone wrong now. Five minutes later, Ty's vehicle pulled up, and exiting quickly, he joined the others. He and Aaron had a serious chat, their expressions anxious as they glanced her way. Climbing to her feet, she trusted her shaky legs enough to cross the lawn and join them. "How much of the house is ruined?"

Ty put a hand on her shoulder. "Just the two bedrooms and part of the hall. We were lucky you found it so soon. The rest looks okay." He met her gaze. "Can you tell me exactly what you saw driving home?"

"Just flames and some smoke. I pulled over next door to call the station, then I came here to try and tamp down as much as I could. That's about it."

"Did you pass anyone on the road?" Ty asked, his worried expression surprising her. "Think hard. It's important. Anyone, even neighbors."

Running it back through her memory, she said, "No. Not since I turned off the main road." She stared at their tense faces. "Why? What's wrong? You're scaring me."

Aaron moved to put a reassuring arm around her shoulders. "I'm sorry, honey. We found a body inside."

It took a moment for his words to sink in. Struggling to make sense of the information, she asked, "Whose body would be inside? You and I are the only ones who are ever there." She began to shake and clutched at him for support. "Your family—"

"It's not either of them. I just texted them both and got replies right away." He met her gaze. "We think it might be Stacy Metters. One of the guys just found her car parked behind the barn."

She felt like her brain had seeped out her ears as she tried to take it all in. "What do you mean? Why on earth would she be here?"

"Maybe our arsonist killed her somewhere else and brought her here." He shrugged, then tightened his hold. "Ty and his officers will have to guard the house until the ashes cool enough to allow a closer examination. It appears that the fire started near her body."

"W-was she already dead?"

She saw the guarded look from him to Ty before he answered. "I'm sorry, I don't know. Try not to think about it." How could she not? She knew how terrified she'd been when surrounded by flames and knew the damage that could be wrought by them. The fact that she hadn't liked Stacy didn't mean she would wish a painful death like this on her or anyone for that matter. She sucked in a groan and couldn't stop the tears that followed. Aaron lowered himself into one of the patio chairs and pulled her onto his lap, cradling her as everyone around them continued to work.

After she pulled herself together, she encouraged him to go back to work. In an effort to keep herself occupied, she made coffee up at the cottage for the men still working, rustling up some cookies for those who needed a bite to keep them going. Most of them finally packed it in, leaving one man to guard the site until they could take a closer look in the morning. Since the weather was supposed to stay fine for a few days and the sky was currently clear, they would wait until morning to put tarps over the damage. The ashes would have cooled by then and they could fully examine the scene. In the clear light of day, they would make their determinations and then protect that side of the house until it could be repaired. Thank God for house insurance.

Harper watched as Ty pulled Aaron into a corner and they had a long chat. There were no smiles in sight. The fact that the arsonist had taken his crimes to a whole new level terrified all of them. Now, other lives might be at stake. Stacy had paid a terrible price.

She and Aaron retired to her cottage for the rest of the night, realizing this would be their place to sleep for the time being. He guided her gently, removing both their clothes before heading to the shower. It was a relief to have someone take over. The act of him massaging shampoo into her hair proved oddly soothing. Washing her as one would a child, he took care of his own needs next, then wrapped a large towel around each of them. He dried them both off, then tucked her into bed, climbing in beside her. "You should call your mother," she suggested. "I don't want her to worry."

"I texted her again a while ago. She knows we're okay and she filled Sammy in on the updates. She said they'll be over to check on us first thing in the morning."

That should have reassured her. Instead, she wrapped her arms around his waist, buried her cheek into his shoulder and let the tears come once again. Both relief and stress caused it, she knew, but she needed to let all the tension out. Afterward, she sighed. "I'm so sorry about your house."

"That's the least of my worries. Houses can be rebuilt," he murmured. "I have faith that we'll find him and we'll stop him. He's losing control or he wouldn't have done such a terrible thing. We just have to figure out how Stacy was involved."

It was the last thing she remembered him saying before she fell asleep. When she woke in the morning, the sheets on his side of the bed were cold. *How long has he been up?* Stretching, she flipped the covers back and stood. Faint voices drifted up to her. Moving to the window, she peered down the slope. Ty stood talking with Aaron and his mother. If Sammy had come along as they'd planned, she was gone now. She must have already left for work.

The only other people she could see were a few men coming and going from the house. A moment later, a gurney appeared, the ravaged body it bore out of sight, encased in a body bag. Just imagining its appearance upset her. She could never be a medical examiner. With a sobering air, the others watched with her as they loaded it up and drove away. Apparently, the ashes had cooled enough to remove the remains and continue the investigation.

She forced herself into the shower, still feeling worn out, as if every bit of energy had drained away. Freshening up and dressing in clean clothes helped a little. When she ventured out to the den, Meredith waited on the couch. Standing, she said, "You poor thing. I'm so sorry about all this. Are you okay?"

Her kind words were all it took to prompt a new bout of tears. Meredith simply let her get it out of her system and pulled her in for a warm hug. She tried to remember the last time anyone except Aaron had hugged her. After she calmed, she pulled away, struggling for a smile. "Just a stress cry. To be honest, I feel ridiculous for being so shaky when such an awful thing happened to Stacy. Do they know anything more about what happened?"

She shook her head. "I came up to see you, because they were removing the body. She was a bit of a pain, but it was still too ghastly for me to watch. The autopsy should tell us something that could help, I would think."

"I hope so."

"Sammy had to go to work, but she said to get extra rest and she'll check in later."

"That's sweet of her. I'm so sorry I missed her."

"Aaron wanted you to get some sleep. Don't worry. There's plenty of time for all of us to hang out." She clasped her hand. "Would you like to come and stay with me for a while? You're welcome to, if you need to get away. I have plenty of room."

They both sat and she felt better with the additional support. Frowning, she said, "I appreciate the thought, but I seem to be bringing bad luck to everyone around me. It makes me paranoid, like having me around is bad luck."

"Don't say that. I have a son who thinks you're the very best kind of luck. This monster is the only one to blame, not you." She gently squeezed her fingers. "I don't think you realize how much you've added to my son's life. I've never seen him this happy outside the firehouse." The sweet words lifted her depressed mood. When they resumed talking about their situation, she felt much calmer. Ultimately, they decided she would be safest staying with Aaron, but his mother's kindness touched her and made her feel welcome in their family circle. Meredith left with a wave, promising to return soon.

Watching out the window, she saw Aaron gesture toward the back of the house and watched as the group of men pulled tarps from the back of Ty's truck. As they toiled, she made some fresh biscuits to go with the brew and offered them to the men when they were finished working. Everyone smiled and nodded their thanks, then disappeared shortly after, moving on to catch up with their regular workday. That was what she liked about this small town; many people pitched in to help anyone in need.

The tiring day passed in a blur. Her only time away from the cottage was her first physiotherapy appointment. She did the best she could, but the events of the previous night had tired her. When she explained the situation and they realized who she was, the staff exercised more patience. Aaron had to go to work, but after she returned home, she just couldn't concentrate on her projects. She caught up on some extra sleep instead. He woke her when he came home a little earlier than normal and headed for the shower. Soon after, she heard a noise outside and went to investigate. An exhausted Ty showed up on the porch, wiping his feet on the mat. "Can I come in?" he asked when she greeted him. In answer, she swung the door wide for him to enter.

"Aaron's just getting showered and changed. He'll be out in a minute." She followed him inside and waved him to an armchair. He sank into it with a grateful sigh. In turn, she perched on the arm of the couch, still feeling jittery. "Do you have any news?"

"Yes, but I want to wait for him so I don't have to go through it twice. My energy's at low ebb at the moment."

"You need some sleep." The pronounced circles under his eyes made him look like he'd applied cheap, smudged mascara to his tanned skin.

"That sounds like the same sermon I got from my wife earlier. You guys aren't ganging up on me, are you?" He forced a grin. "Don't worry. I'll grab a few hours after I'm done here."

When Aaron came through the bedroom door, he settled next to her on the couch, his arm resting against her back. Ty cleared his throat. "According to our latest information, it appears that Stacy came here of her own volition."

Aaron ran a hand through his still-damp hair. "Why in hell would she come to my place? She's never been here before and I certainly didn't invite her. I don't even know how she got inside."

"Well, I finally tracked down her best friend, Tammi

Sue Carlton. Apparently, Stacy told her she was going to wait in your bed as a surprise for when you returned home. She even purchased special lingerie in Springvale for the big event."

Harper thought about how pathetic and sad that would be, to have to force yourself on an unwilling man. "But that makes no sense. I might have been in the house. I'm sure everyone in town knows that we're together by now."

"She probably checked to make sure you weren't around. Anyway, I don't think that mattered to her one way or the other. Tammi Sue admitted that if you'd found her, Stacy was going to pretend that she and Aaron had already been together and she just hadn't left yet." He shrugged. "It doesn't make much sense to me, but you know Stacy. Harebrained schemes were her middle name, although I probably shouldn't speak ill of the dead."

The whole thought of what the misguided woman had found waiting instead of pleasure depressed Harper. "Do you think she walked in on the arsonist?"

Ty scratched his head. "Or the other way around. I'm not sure. We'll have to see if the forensics will yield any clues." He came to his feet, swallowing a yawn. "Well, I'm off to grab a few hours of sleep before I turn into a zombie. Stacy's parents were notified by someone in their local department and they'll be here in town tomorrow, looking for answers. Not sure I'll have anything to tell them."

Turning to leave, he paused. "Oh, with all the excitement, I forgot to tell you something. I filed the report about Chief Johnson harassing Harper with the state fire investigator's board. They told me, in confidence, that they will be taking action immediately. Apparently, that was just one complaint too many about him and they're making it a top priority."

"Thank goodness. If they really succeed, we won't be the only ones who are grateful. His own town would be thrilled to see the end of him."

After Ty said his goodbyes, then left, they went to bed early, content to just hold each other and talk. Neither slept well. She could hear him mumble throughout the night as she tossed and turned.

Early the next morning, Ty showed up again. He came inside, grabbing a cookie from the pottery jar Harper had purchased before filling the coffee mug she handed him. Aaron came to stand beside her, wrapping an arm around her shoulders. "We heard a bit of news from the coroner, Harper. Apparently, Stacy's hyoid bone was broken which means she was likely strangled. And there was no smoke in her lungs, either. That means she was dead before the fire started."

"A small blessing, I suppose. Maybe the fact that she didn't suffer will comfort her parents." Her lip quivered, but she held back another bout of tears. "Have they shown up yet?"

"They're due any time now, so I'd better get back to the station." She transferred his coffee to a to-go cup and topped it off. Thanking her, he made his exit.

Aaron paced back and forth until the repetitive motion almost drove her mad. "I don't want you left alone, even for a moment. Not until we catch this maniac."

"I know this is all very upsetting, but—"

He stopped, grasping her forearms, one in each hand. "What if it had been you lying in the embers? I'd never forgive myself."

"Luckily, it wasn't me." She took a shaky breath. "We have to take more precautions, I agree. But finding him could take months and neither one of us can live in a prison. We have responsibilities."

"You don't understand." Pausing, his expression intent, he said, "I love you, Harper." He'd never said it before, even though he'd felt the certainty of it for a while. What they'd been through in the past weeks had convinced him not to wait a moment longer.

Relaxing enough to smile, she replied, "I love you, too."

"Yeah?" An answering grin spread across his face. "How about that? I really needed some great news right about now."

She put one hand up against his cheek, relishing the warmth of his skin. "We'll figure out a plan to keep safe, one that lets us do our jobs and stay protected. And, one day soon, we'll catch this bastard."

"Okay," he said, sighing. "Let's do that. You keep reading that diary. Ty and I will knuckle down on the evidence we've collected, no matter how thin. Amongst all that information, there's got to be a clue somewhere that we missed."

She selfishly wanted life to return to her new normal. The original fire had, strangely, made a personal life with Aaron seem more possible. Worrying that she had unwittingly made Aaron a target made the contents of her stomach rock. Would his family ever forgive her if something happened to him?

She did the dishes, taking her frustration out on scrubbing the pots to keep her mind on other things.

Chapter Sixteen

Over the next few days, Harper tried to distract herself to keep from worrying too much. Everyone stayed busy, especially Aaron. Repairing the house began almost immediately, which was great, although the constant banging of hammers nearly drove the two of them insane. The nylon tarps were soon replaced with exterior walls that had to have siding repaired. The work on the inside followed. Thank goodness, at that point, the racket became more muffled. At first, Aaron attempted to continue work as usual, but he said his mind kept searching for answers to the crimes. She knew exactly how he felt. Even her stock was getting precariously low due to brisk online sales and reduced work hours because of all the fuss.

Aaron worked his usual shifts, but he called almost hourly and insisted on coming home at lunch to check on her. Harper thought it excessive and told him so, but she didn't push him about it, which he appreciated. On some level, it reassured him, so she agreed it wasn't worth arguing about. When she went to her therapy appointments, he made her call when she left and after she returned. He wasn't sleeping well, either, and she knew he was always considering the nightmarish possibilities. Ty had men working overtime, but no new clues had surfaced. Aaron had been discussing the crimes with state fire investigators. If there wasn't a break in the case soon, he told her he would have to formally request their onsite assistance. She knew it was the last thing he wanted, but the ongoing threat may not leave him with any other choice.

****

When Aaron found a spare minute during the day, he phoned and told Ty about his recent visit to warn off Sutton. They'd been so busy lately with other things, he hadn't mentioned it. In response, his friend whistled, then said, "I know it must have been tempting, but you didn't lay a hand on him, did you? Might be a little hard to explain away a fat lip and a black eye."

"You know me better than that. I just made it clear that if it happens again, I'm bringing charges against him. I also pointed out the potential damage to his career."

"I'm sure he appreciated that. Can't say I blame you, though. If it was Sandra, I'd have done the same thing." He grinned. "Do you think that's enough to keep him away?"

"I hope so. I don't need any more distractions right now."

He agreed. "With him, Chief Johnson and all the other suspects, I'd say we have more than our share of problems to deal with." Saying goodbye, he hung up, leaving Aaron to get back to work.

****

Pacing back and forth in his living room, the arsonist tried to dredge up some measure of sorrow at having committed murder. The actual deed of throttling the little bitch should have repulsed him. Instead, tightening his fingers around that slut's neck had felt divine, as if the outcome was inevitable from the start. And her look of

163

disbelief when she recognized him made him smile as he drank in her very last gasp and memorized every nuance. If only he could have filmed it, to relive the experience over and over again.

He'd had sex with her, a year or two ago, as had almost every man in town. She'd been an exercise of physical release, nothing more. A vessel, as it were. He'd forgotten her meaningless existence the moment he was done. The stupid bitch had simply been in the wrong place at the wrong time. That wasn't his fault. He didn't invite her to come along on his quest. Aaron had turned her down sexually time after time and she still thought waiting in his bed was a winning plan. Didn't she know that men always want what they can't have? The easiest women are used and then thrown out like the trash they're named after, abandoned in the street.

He'd approached Aaron's house through the overgrown back pasture, skirting the trees that were always his shelter. His backpack and gasoline can were his only companions. Observing the surroundings for some time proved to him that no one was around. Afterward, he'd settled back in the same place for a short while to enjoy the drama. Watching from the shelter of the woods, he'd seen Harper's frantic approach, as well as her pathetic efforts to douse the growing flames. He'd been tempted to ambush her, but knew the timing wouldn't work in his favor.

Not long after his feat, he'd made sure he was seen on the other side of town, demonstrating signs of shock and dismay at the news. He was already dreaming up the daring plan for Harper's demise. This fire had been meant as a simple distraction, before Stacy entered the picture and complicated things. He needed the firemen and sheriff's deputies all out of sorts, distracted, before he struck the ultimate blow. There was only a small force here and few firefighters, so, now, they were pulled in a million different directions. He would strike while they floundered.

By a stroke of luck, he'd overheard Ty and Aaron at the diner talking about a diary over lunch. They wanted Harper to read through it, to look for clues. Their words puzzled him. The question was, whose diary was it? It couldn't be her mother's. If her mother had left a diary, he would have been aware of it long before now.

Wouldn't he?

\*\*\*\*

For what felt like the hundredth night, Harper sat curled on the sofa, reading. It was a relief to be back in the house so soon. Between volunteers and a few paid workers, the repairs had been done in record time. Tonight, Aaron had to go back into the firehouse, because one man had to go home sick and the substitute couldn't get there until later. She decided to stay put, locking the door behind him, to head back to scouring the journal for clues. Wondering whether she'd already missed something important put a knot in her stomach, but she pressed ahead. A short while later, her tired eyes jerked to a stop on the fourth line of her current page. Disbelief had her reading the words twice, surprise making her focus harder on the faint, scrawled words.

The diary read; *I'm so weak now. What will happen to my beautiful little girl? J used his hospital privileges to stand and stare at me from the doorway, saying nothing. The look in his eyes frightened me. How can a doctor do the terrible things he has done?*

She huffed in a breath, panic seizing her body. One

name stood at the forefront of her thoughts. It was Dr. Mason—it had to be. Educated, intense, sophisticated…and he was the only doctor around she knew of who was the right age. She wanted to vomit, remembering how often he'd been right beside her as she recovered in the hospital. Never questioning his professionalism, she'd been grateful for his excellent care. When she'd looked up his name under the hospital website, though, his middle name was William, his first Phillip. It had caused her to cross him off the list of her mother's potential lovers. Was she reaching too far? Why would her mother refer to him as J? Maybe the J reference wasn't a name, but a nickname. Grabbing her cellphone, she forced her shaking fingers to call Aaron. She had to tell him what she'd uncovered. If he thought she was getting excited over nothing, she'd just keep searching.

No answer at the other end meant the messaging system clicked on. Was he at a fire? She couldn't leave something like this in a message. A rare sense of urgency had her pulling on her sneakers, her trembling fingers fumbling to tie them and then grabbing her keys. She would drive straight to the fire station. If he wasn't there, she could always go and discuss this strong potential lead with Ty. Perhaps, later, they would laugh together about the faulty conclusions she'd drawn, but for now, she wasn't taking any chances. If it was him, he might be planning to start a fire tonight. Her information might be the only thing that would stop him. Lunging for the front door, she swung it open, letting it bang against the wall in her haste.

Time seemed to move in slow motion. Recognizing the face of the man waiting on the stoop, she scrambled to leap back and slam the door shut, in a futile attempt to squeeze him back out as he advanced. *Too late.* Her weakened arm gave way as she clawed at the doorframe. "Oh, Harper," he murmured, shoving her back so he could enter. "There you are." Grabbing her and holding her in a choke hold, he promised, "At long last, the time for your grand finale has finally come." A painful pinch in her arm caused her to yelp out loud. The lights faded as her body slumped, skidding down the wall. Her muscles refused to work and the last thing she remembered was sliding to the cold, tile floor.

\*\*\*\*

Taking his mask off, Aaron swept a hand over his sweaty face, feeling the mess from outside of the mask lines spread over his heated skin. The barn fire had taken every available man, but it was finally out, thank goodness. At least the structure was abandoned, so there'd been no loss of life this time, either animal or human. Pausing to hand everyone a bottle of water, he said, "Ten-minute break and then let's finish up with this mess and go home."

Rocky came lumbering over, sipping his drink. "Our arsonist at work again?"

"I'm pretty sure. From what I can see, there's multiple points of origin, anyway. I guess we'll know for sure tomorrow after everything cools off. No injuries or fatalities, so we'll be thankful for that." They took a few minutes' break, shaking their heads at the piles of ashes and charred chunks of wood which remained. After their return to their duties, it only took twenty minutes to take care of everything and render it safe. Most of the team headed back to get some sleep. He posted one man and a small pump truck to stay until morning, just to be sure nothing sparked back to life. Traveling back to the station, he let Rocky drive and texted Harper. No answer concerned him until he checked his watch. *Almost midnight.* She was probably tired of waiting for him and had fallen asleep.

He stopped to have a brief word with everyone back at the station and then headed home for a long, hot shower before bed. Hopefully, Harper would be curled up in his bed and he could just slide in beside her. It was now his favorite place to be. Fatigue slowed his thoughts and he concentrated on getting home safely. Pulling in the driveway ten minutes later, he was surprised to see the living room lights shining through the front window. The sight made him smile. Maybe she'd awakened and decided to wait up for him.

That feeling of contentment lasted until he rounded the corner of the house and spied the wide-open front door. Alarm followed a moment of confusion. Throwing the truck in park, he took five running steps to launch through the door, leaving the truck door open and the engine running. "Harper!" No one answered.

Premonition shook him and he yelled her name again. He took undeniable risks, racing through the house without regard to his safety, only to find the empty rooms told a terrifying story. The small front table he left his keys on was knocked out of place. On second look at the front door, he found claw marks in the paint on the wall by the light switch, telling gouges that hadn't been there that morning. Stomach churning, he called Ty. As soon as his sleepy voice answered, Aaron spat out, "She's gone!"

"Who? Harper?"

His heart hammering in his chest, he shouted, "Get

over here. Someone took her."

****

When Harper regained consciousness, her head pounded as if caught in a metal vise. *Where am I?* Nausea mingled with a profound dizziness. The last time she'd found herself in this position, she'd been in a fire, but there were no flames to threaten her now. She cautiously raised her head. A beautiful mahogany coffee table in front of her swam into focus as well as the details of an intricate Persian carpet at her feet. *What the hell?*

"You're awake." She recognized the deep, male voice that sounded preternaturally calm. Swiveling her head toward the sound caused a stabbing shaft of pain, making her wince. She gazed, blinking, at the slender man sitting opposite the couch on which she lay. Dr. Mason glared back at her, his penetrating gaze unnerving. A memory of the diary and its damning contents came back in a rush. Her instincts had been right, but what good would that information do her now?

"It's you." A part of her had been unable to believe the suave man was behind all this chaos, but undeniable evidence lay before her. Any possible motivation for his crimes evaded her.

"Yes, Harper, it's me. It's always been me." His bitter tone further confused her.

"I don't understand." She struggled to even form the words. "Why? What have I ever done to you?"

He leapt to his feet. "You took her away from me!" Her innocent words seemed to turn a switch. She saw the madness now in his eyes, an astounding lack of humanity in the emptiness that waited there. It stole her breath.

She struggled for calm, her mind reeling. Panicking now would only get her killed that much quicker. Trying to reason with him, she said, "I wasn't even born when my mother broke up with you. I had nothing to do with her decision."

His narrowed gaze pinned her in place. "Maybe not, but you still managed to lure her away from me. People like you are evil from conception." He paced back and forth, powered by a manic frenzy. The motion made her want to close her eyes, but she didn't dare. He could strike a fatal blow without warning, she thought, thinking of Stacy. His voice mimicked a female tone. "I have to think about the baby. I have to do what's right." In a flash, his tone returned to normal. "What about me? Why didn't anyone care about what was right for me?"

What could she say that wouldn't egg him on? "I'm certain that my mother loved you."

"Not enough." A chopping motion with his hand underscored his point. "Not enough to leave you behind. I thought once you were born, she'd change her mind. But no, you were a filthy, squalling infant and she still dared to choose you over me."

Her thoughts milled as she struggled to think of what to say. How would she buy enough time to give Aaron a chance to find her? Precious seconds were ticking away. "She knew you didn't want children, but she did."

"She was supposed to love me, not some whining brat. I said I'd be happy to pay for an abortion, but she wouldn't hear of it." Leaning over, he grabbed her arm and shouted the next words. "She called me a monster. A monster! All I ever did was love her." He paused to loom over her, spit gathering in the corners of his mouth. "Why couldn't you just die?"

Chapter Seventeen

Aaron watched through the front window of his house as Ty's red pickup screeched to a halt by the front door, scattering gravel. He bounded out and entered the house in a rush. "Did you find anything?"

Panic shortened his breath. "No. I don't—where would this maniac take her?"

"Take a minute to calm down. Breathe." He put a hand on his arm and squeezed. "Now, think. What had she found out so far? He was educated and we're assuming his name started with J, right?"

"Yes. She found references to him being sophisticated and intense, too." Aaron's gaze stopped at the coffee table and hurried to search through the papers there.

"What are you doing?"

"The diary's gone. It was right here. Maybe he took it or she moved it, but, sometimes, she took notes." He plucked a tattered page from the pile. "Educated. Sophisticated. Does name start with J?" He gulped in a breath. "She wrote down a note. It says, 'Could J be a middle name or a nickname?'"

"Maybe. She's got a point." He turned and met Aaron's gaze. "Your mom's about the same age as Harper's mom would have been if she'd lived, right? Call and ask her if she knows anyone with that nickname or middle name. A professional of some kind."

"I asked her about it once."

"Ask her again. Maybe she's had some time to think about it."

He grabbed his cellphone and punched her number on the auto dial. It seemed to take forever before her sleepy voice said, "Are you okay?"

"This is urgent, Mom. Don't ask why—I'll tell you later. I know I asked about a man with a first or last name starting with J before. I need you to think about it again." He twitched, unable to keep still as he talked. "It may not be a first name. Do you remember a man with the nickname or middle name of J? Remember, not necessarily J-A-Y. Any name that involves the letter J." He ran out of breath and gulped in some air. "He's likely a doctor, a lawyer, a professional of some sort." He turned on the speaker phone so Ty could also hear her response.

"Oh, my goodness. Let me wake up enough to think." Aaron could practically hear a metronome, counting down the final moments of Harper's life. "I already gave you the list of the people I could think of." He started to lose hope. "Well…wait a second. I remember they used to call Dr. Mason that years ago. His mother used to call him J and say it was short for juvenile delinquent. I think after she lost her other son, she went a little nuts. Unfortunately, the nickname caught on and he got bullied a lot about it."

"You're sure?"

"Of course…Oh, God help us. Is that—"

His pulse doubling, he thanked her and hung up while she was still sputtering questions. Could it really be that simple?

"I know where he lives," Ty muttered, rushing for

the door. In their panic, they left his door wide open. "We can call for help on the way." Aaron clambered in beside him, hearing the engine roar to life. They rocketed down the drive and, tires screaming, bulleted down the road.

Overwhelming dread pinched his stomach. "What if she's not there? What if he has her somewhere else?" And, then, the inevitable question struck him…what if they were wrong and they were wasting precious time on the wrong man? He repeated that terrifying thought to Ty.

"Then we'll deal with that when we come to it. At this moment, it feels right." He called the station, getting more men to help. "Ten minutes, Aaron. Ten minutes and we'll be there."

The short drive felt like it took hours, the time ticking like a bomb in his head. His heart pounded a rhythm that matched the racing engine. When at last they arrived on the doctor's street, Ty cut the truck's headlights and slowed to a crawl. Five houses down, the large, modern, white brick house sat on an upward slope, elegant pillars marking the entrance. From the front perspective, the property appeared to be deserted, but he likely kept his car in the garage out back. When they advanced to the far side, however, they could see blazing lights switched on in the rear of the house. Parking on the shoulder of the road, Ty turned to him. "We can stay tight against the house and see if we can hear anything or see through a window. Don't make a move until I say go, okay? We don't know exactly who or what we're dealing with."

"Done." He would save her whatever the cost, take a chance by offering his life for hers. This sick bastard wasn't going to take her away from him. Ty radioed his men that they were evaluating the scene and cautioned them to approach with care. Easing out the door, Aaron joined him at the front bumper of the truck. As they turned to start creeping up the drive, Aaron heard a heartrending shriek. Recognizing Harper's voice, he abandoned all pretense of staying quiet and raced up the paved slope, Ty in hot pursuit.

****

"You don't have to do this," Harper pleaded, working her bleeding wrists back and forth against the rope that bound her hands behind her back. The healing injury throbbed, reminding her that her compromised strength might hinder her.

Mason splashed the gasoline on the floor to set the stage for a wide circle of flames that would eventually come at her from all sides, leaving her no escape. The overpowering stench burned her nostrils. "You haven't given me any choice. You just refused to die. I can't be whole again until I've destroyed you."

Struggling to think of anything that would slow the hopeless descent to destruction, she said, "My mother wouldn't want you to do this. She loved both of us." She had to stop him before he went much further. "And the sheriff will know it was you, anyway. He and Aaron have gathered a lot more evidence than you think."

Pausing for a moment, he grinned, the macabre twist of his mouth warping his handsome face. "Oh, poor me. My lovely home has just become the latest victim of the arsonist. And I have no idea why he chose to end your life here. Who could have imagined such an unforeseen tragedy?"

"You think you're so much smarter than they are, but you're not. They'll know it was you. I left behind notes I made after reading the diary." If he'd looked for the diary, he'd have found it tucked under the arm of the sofa, but he hadn't taken the time.

He sneered, looking more like an arrogant teenager than the man she thought she knew. "They don't have a clue about what I've done or they would have arrested me by now. I'm a damned pillar of this community. You, on the other hand, are a nobody." Sticking out his chest, he lifted his chin and said, "They never had a clue about what happened to your father, even back then. They never even glanced in my direction."

Trepidation stiffened her spine as she tried to make sense of his words. "What do you mean? What do you know about my dad?"

"You thought your father ran off, didn't you? Well, he did, but he was coming back for you once he put the pieces together." His gaze met hers, his eyes gleaming with triumph. "Nobody would have guessed that, of all people, he would be the one to figure it out. His IQ was probably half of mine. But I was there to stop him and he never saw the end coming until it was too late to defeat me." He swung his arms wide, sloshing the gasoline. "The fool. He paid for his stupidity with his life. Who's the winner now?"

She tried to work past the crushing pain in her chest. *I can't think about what he revealed. If I do, I won't survive.* She envisioned Aaron telling her to fight in any way she could. Renewing the tussle with her hands, blinking back the pain, she felt a few strands unravelling. One of her hands popped free and she almost cried out in relief. Rubbing her wrist against her back, she stifled a groan as blood flowed once again, making her fingers ache and tingle. When he turned back to his job, she gauged the distance from her position to the door. Could she leap across the room in time? *Either that or die trying.* She'd run out of options, the chance to survive petering down to mere seconds.

When he doused the far side of the room with gasoline, she leapt to her feet and ran. Her socked feet worked on the carpet, but skittered and slid as she reached the section of hardwood floor. She heard the devil chasing behind her, cursing. Her hand landed hard on the doorknob, only to be jerked back off as he snatched her from behind, his claw-like arms clamped around her waist. "Help! Please!" she screamed, battling his desperate grasp.

He dragged her back half the distance of the room, his strong arms an impossible barrier. Pinned against him, she couldn't act to save herself. As she struggled, she heard glass shatter and, like an avenging god, Aaron vaulted through the splintered door. With a roar of rage, he lunged across the room to confront them. Yanking her out of Mason's arms, he thrust her to one side. He punched Mason in the jaw, but the other man recovered and came back, swinging. Suddenly, Ty was beside her, shoving her toward the exit. "Get outside," he shouted over the racket. "Help is coming."

She did as he asked, but stayed just outside the door, watching and listening as approaching sirens rent the air. Mason had struggled free and escaped to the other side of the room. Now, the three men had come to a standoff. Aaron and Ty faced the demented doctor from a dozen feet away. She couldn't figure out why they didn't tackle him until she saw the lighter now in his hands. Ty raised his voice, the tone of the words amazingly calm. "Come on, Mason. There's no way out. Put down the gasoline and the lighter. No one needs to get hurt."

"She's evil," he shrieked, his body spasming with rage. Hatred oozed from every pore as he swung the lighter back and forth in his clasped fist. "No one but I can see what she really is. She stole my life away. She ruined everything!"

Ty's gaze followed his movements, his legs staggered as if braced to run. Aaron stayed beside him. "You have a good job, a nice home, your health. You can come back from this. There's a lot to be grateful for." He stood stock still, his voice attempting to soothe.

Mason's eyes raged, his torment darkening them to near black. "I'm alone. I'm always alone. She took away thc only person who ever loved me."

Harper saw the moment when the men realized they were standing too close to him. Now that she was safe, they edged back toward the door a few paces, still trying to calm him enough for him to give himself up.

Rushing two quick paces to the left, he suddenly lit the lighter and, with a cry of triumph, dropped it at his feet. Flame burst all around him, climbing his clothes and making an unholy halo of fire that engulfed the man in mere seconds. Aaron and Ty ran out the door, gathering her to drag her farther away from the conflagration. Waving the newly arrived firemen forward as they donned their masks, Aaron stood back to let them lead with the heavy hose spraying. They could advance no farther than the door as they faced down the wall of flames.

Sobbing, she let Ty hold her to one side as Aaron helped the vigilant men fight the leaping flames in an attempt to limit the destruction. The house might be a loss, but they could fight to save the neighbor's houses.

The EMTs who'd just arrived insisted on checking her out. Ty and his deputies stood by, ready to assist however they could. After a brief examination, the medical team decided she should be assessed and treated at the hospital. "I won't leave until the flames are out and I know everyone's safe." She crossed her arms and planted her feet. They grudgingly allowed her to stay until then.

Thirty minutes later, after the men managed to get the fire under control, Aaron took his mask off and kissed her. The spots his mask didn't cover were blackened and left a mark on her cheek that he tried to rub away with his fingers. "Time for you to go and let a doctor make sure you're okay. I'll be there as soon as I can."

Knowing it was a fruitless question, she still felt compelled to ask. "Is he—"

Aaron squeezed her hand, his eyes somber. "He's gone. He never had a chance to survive and he knew it. He chose his end."

She brushed away useless tears for the nemesis who'd despised her. "How did you find out where I was?"

"I'll tell you after you get cleared to go home." She didn't push her luck, going sedately along with the ambulance team. After her arrival, they treated her wrists, x-raying the newly healed one to be certain she hadn't reinjured it. By some miracle, she hadn't. Apparently, the rough treatment had caused some swelling. They put ice packs around it to reduce the aggravation caused by her escape. Some pain pills were supplied to give her relief. Otherwise, she was shaken but okay. The blood technician took a sample to determine which drug she'd been given so they could assess any potential long-term damage and include the information in her victim statement. Bruises and cuts were the least of her worries, simply cleaned and bandaged. She couldn't believe she had survived another fire virtually unscathed.

When the men arrived, she told Ty the basics of her ordeal. He said she could come in the next morning to fill out the victim's statement after she got a decent sleep. Finding Aaron and his family waiting in the visitor's lounge, she let them cradle and soothe her, relishing the fact that it didn't feel awkward at all. The entire hospital crew had heard the horrible report about what had happened and they were in shock. The hospital board was notified so they could deal with the public relations nightmare of the killer being one of their own staff members. After Aaron's sister and mother assured themselves that everyone had survived intact, they headed home.

By the time she and Aaron arrived at their place, her watch read almost four in the morning. They showered, barely able to stand, and fell into bed, exhaustion claiming them. Wrapping their arms around each other for reassurance, they slept that way until late morning. When they woke, they made slow, lazy love, an affirmation of survival. She had never felt so wanted and needed. Aaron stared into her eyes, as if he couldn't believe she was really there. "I've never been so frightened in my life," he admitted. "I thought we weren't going to reach you in time."

"Me, either. As far as the fear goes, at least. I thought you might find me if I could just keep him talking. Thank God it worked." Still, there was one thing she had to tell him. "There's one revelation I didn't get around to telling you last night. H-he said he killed my father."

'What?" He propped up on one elbow, his eyebrows drawn. "What are you talking about?"

"He said he killed him because he figured out that Mason was the one setting fires. According to him, Dad came back to take me away and he ambushed him."

"He didn't say what happened to his body?"

"No. He didn't even say how he killed him, just that he did." He cuddled her close while she cried for the father she thought had long forgotten her. After a while, she felt calm again, more from simple exhaustion than anything else.

"You realize I may never let you out of this house again?"

She cocked her head, knowing he was trying to distract her and appreciating the effort. "What are you going on about now?"

"Everyone keeps trying to take you away from me," he grumbled. "Arsonists, old boyfriends…"

"That will never happen."

"No?" She propped herself up to see his frown change to a grin. "I like the sound of that."

Having slept longer than expected, they filled out the necessary reports at the sheriff's department in the early afternoon. Everyone around them seemed pretty subdued and who could blame them. Aaron pulled Ty aside and told him about what Mason had said to Harper about her father. They vowed to look into it after the rest of the case was finished. Wherever her father's remains lay, they'd been there for years. Another few days wouldn't make any difference.

Some news stations had reporters waiting to ask for interviews when they exited the building, which they declined. Mason's body had been transported to the morgue, what little there was left of it. Sadly, no one seemed to care about the remains. Although he'd been responsible for his own choices, Harper felt a stab of sadness for him. "It's terrible to have no one who gives a damn about whether you live or die. For a while after my mother passed, that's exactly how I felt."

"You feel sorry for a man who tried to kill you four times?" Aaron raised his eyebrows. "You're a caring person, but that might be taking empathy a little too far."

She understood his streak of protectiveness and cherished it. "It seems crazy to most people, I know. But I know what it's like to feel all alone in the world. It's the hardest thing imaginable."

He sighed. "I guess I see too much selfish behavior, sometimes. He could easily have carried on with his life and found someone else, but he'd rather blame you for what he became. It doesn't make any sense." When she didn't respond, he continued. "You weren't even born when your mother left him, but in his mind, you were the cause of all his miseries. I wonder if he was just born that way."

"Didn't you tell me you found out from your mother that his brother died in a fire?"

"Yes. That's one of the things she told me when I called her, looking for help."

That one fact made her wonder. "Do you think he might have had something to do with that fire, too?"

His surprise turned into a shrug. "Maybe. I might look at the reports just out of interest if they're still around. Maybe his brother's death is what made your dad suspicious. I guess we'll never know."

"Do you need to go to work?"

He shook his head. "There are only a few hours of my workday left and I'm taking it as vacation. The others will call if they need me." They returned to the house, not wanting people gawking at them and gossiping any more than they already had. They took it easy until dinner. After they washed up the dishes afterward, he said, "Want to sit on the deck for a while and relax?"

"Sure. Don't be surprised if I doze off." They ended up curled together on the oversized lawn chair with a light blanket to keep them warm. His body fit against hers like a puzzle, as if they were made to fit together.

After a few minutes, he said, "I want you to move in with me."

She slid onto her back to gaze up at him, smiling. "Really?"

"Yes. Is that something you'd be interested in?"

"Absolutely. I'm pretty much here all the time, anyway." Kissing his cheek, she snuggled against him, chest to chest this time, her head tucked under his chin.

"After all we've been through, lately, I don't want to waste another minute apart."

She lifted her head to stare into his eyes. "And after word gets around town about us moving in together, you won't have to make all those threatening faces at other men anymore."

He smirked. "Don't know what you're talking about."

"Will your family be okay with us living together? I don't want to upset anybody."

"You're kidding, right? My mother had pretty much given up on me finding a partner. She'll probably shoot off some fireworks to celebrate."

\*\*\*\*

Right before bed, Ty called to check in on them and ask him to bring all the information he had about the fires to the station. Aaron put him on speaker phone so they could both hear. "I want to complete this file and move on."

He smiled at Harper. "I think we're all ready for that."

"I did discover one thing we'd missed, though, but I'm not sure of the exact relevance. Did you know that both of Harper's previous fires occurred on the same date?"

"Are you serious?"

"Yup. We must have looked at those reports a dozen times and missed it."

"So, it must have been an anniversary of some kind."

"I'd bet money on it. And the date was October twentieth."

"Yesterday."

"Yes. It wouldn't have changed anything. We still wouldn't have known who was behind it."

"But we might have tightened our security at the time in question."

"That's true, but you know what they say about hindsight." Sighing, he bid them goodnight.

Leaping to her feet, she said, "The diary might tell us." She dug into the side of the sofa and pulled it out.

"The night you were gone, I thought Mason had taken it."

"No. He never saw it, thank goodness." Asking for the date again, she flipped to the very beginning. After some searching, she said, "Oh, my gosh. I can't believe it."

"What?"

Tears came to the corner of her eyes. "It was the date Mom broke up with him. Look."

He took the diary from her and read the relevant passage. It was the anniversary of the greatest pain in Mason's pathetic life. Because he felt Harper's mother had ended his life, he chose to celebrate that anniversary by destroying all that was left of her. It all made a terrible kind of sense.

The next day, Aaron returned to work. Everything had stayed quiet the previous day, for which he was thankful. His men banded around him, asking questions about Mason's part in Stacy's death. For those who hadn't been involved, he told them what had happened, downplaying the horror of seeing a man light himself on fire. He'd take that vision to his grave. It was something he hoped to never witness again. Some of the men had known Mason for years, liked him enough to be shocked at all that had transpired. He thought of all the times men were arrested for terrible things while their neighbors insisted they were good men. It was daunting to know how much evil could be hidden behind closed doors.

Wanting to end the discussion on a more positive note, he told the men about Harper moving in with him. There were the expected hoots and whistles along with congratulatory thumps on the back. She'd won them over with her baked goods and her sweet nature. When the phone rang, he excused himself to answer it, leaving them to enjoy the latest batch of cookies.

At five thirty, Harper stuck her head into his office door. "Hey, handsome."

"What are you doing here?" He'd been thinking about her all day.

"I went for a walk around town to stretch my legs and thought I'd catch a lift home."

"Feeling restless?"

"A little."

He grabbed his coat. "Well, I had some good news this afternoon."

"We can always use more of that."

"The investigators finished their in-depth analysis of Chief Johnson's department and he's being replaced immediately. There are whispers of a long list of criminal charges headed his way. Kickbacks, mishandling of funds and all kinds of trouble."

"That doesn't surprise you, does it?"

"No, but it means his days of harassing Rocky and me are over. Thank goodness. Anything else is up to the lawyers to figure out."

"Who would have guessed that all of our problems would go away within the span of a week?"

"Not me." He grinned. "You must be my good luck charm."

The men called hello to Harper as they passed and she yelled, "Hi, guys," back. Stepping outside into the sun, he helped her into the truck and slammed the door. With a parting glance at the station, he hopped in, started the engine and headed back to the only place they wanted to be tonight. Home.

## A word about the author…

Dianne McCartney is an award-winning writer, speaker and contest judge from Canon City, Colorado. She lives with her husband, Mitch, among the deer, coyotes and other wildlife. Her novels are mainstream thriller/suspense and contemporary romance published by The Wild Rose Press. Her latest release, Dark Venom, is the third book in The Elijah Black Trilogy. She has sixty-eight writing awards from contests in Oklahoma and Texas and is a long-standing member of the OWFI and The Rose Rock Writers. She's also a member of Sisters In Crime, The Tornado Alley Mystery Writers and The Oklahoma Romance Writers Guild. http://www.diannemccartney.com